MORNING
CHILD

MORNING CHILD

HAROLD MYRA

ZondervanPublishingHouse
Grand Rapids, Michigan

A Division of HarperCollins*Publishers*

Morning Child
Copyright © 1994 by Harold Myra
All rights reserved

Requests for information should be addressed to:
Zondervan Publishing House
Grand Rapids, Michigan 49530

Library of Congress Cataloging-in-Publication Data

Myra, Harold Lawrence, 1939–
Morning Child / Harold Myra.
p.   cm.
Sequel to: The shining face.
ISBN 0-310-46221-5
I. Title.
PS3563.Y7M67   1994

813'.54—dc20   94-18533
                                                CIP

Cover illustration by Tom Bookwalter
Cover design by Ken Karsen

93 94 95 96 97 98 /❖DH/ 10 9 8 7 6 5 4 3 2 1

For Mandy
and all her family

Contents

PART ONE

────── CHAPTER 1. 11 ──────

The Kitchen   The Quake

The Royal Family   Old Festik

CHAPTER 2. 27

The Welcome Catastrophe   The Red-Haired Child

Earthworms   The Lower Vaults

The Babe in Arms

CHAPTER 3. 45

Traders   In the City   The Strange Visitor

Refuse Heaps   A Little Violence

CHAPTER 4. 63

The Peak   The Trail   The Border

Geysers

PART TWO

────── CHAPTER 5. 87 ──────

Anarchy   Slippery Bodies   The Dais of Light

Golden Hair   Ceremonies   First Night

CHAPTER 6. 107

Skills from the Past   Mysteries   Night Raid

The Loft

CHAPTER 7.   123
That Great, Dark City   Sacred Fire
News from the Front · Proclamations

CHAPTER 8.   139
Swamps   The Queen's Mercy

CHAPTER 9.   151
A Soft Look?   Horses   Home

—— PART THREE ——

CHAPTER 10.   161
Cataclysm   A Withered Little Soul   The Sea
Rags   The Fertile Void   The Feast   Glory

Part One

The shining ones come in strange ways,
and to the least likely of all. . . .

— AN OLD ASKIRIT SAYING

Chapter 1.

—— The Kitchen ——

Bren nervously aligned his military loops as he approached the Royal House and nearly fell over the old man sprawled in the scullery entrance. A ragged arm leaped out, and a bony hand clamped on the young soldier's ankle. "Why the hurry?"

Bren stepped back, ready to jerk his foot out of the man's firm grip. "I have an urgent mission."

"An urgent mission to the kitchen?" The man laughed. "Judgment is upon us, the world is soon to be shattered, and you have an urgent mission to the kitchen." His hearty laughter died into a grim chuckle as he released Bren's ankle but locked his gaze on his face.

Bren averted his eyes, realizing this must be Josk, bearer of dire warnings and barely tolerated by the queen. He had no stomach for confronting him, so he apologized and started forward.

"Stop!"

The old eccentric's command froze Bren.

"Can't you feel the tremors? You mean you're just going to rush in there and not even look at kelerai?"

The rumblings beneath the ground were building, and Bren knew the massive spouts from the oceans below would soon erupt.

But kelerai had exploded into the world every day for centuries, and he was anxious to obey his orders. A common soldier did not make his commander wait.

"Turn around! Stand, boy, and watch." Josk was on his feet as the nine geysers, each like a huge angular pond in the distance, burst from the ground and toward the clouds in a thunderous roar.

Bren did feel awed by it and said, "When kelerai first leaps out like that, I feel it's about to drown me and the whole world." He held up his hands to feel the mist blowing toward them. "But when the birds rise with it, singing, and the sun breaks the spray into rainbows, I feel I'm being lifted into it."

The old man's hand was on Bren's shoulder. "Appreciate kelerai now," he warned. "Soon everyone who draws breath will gasp as the world flies apart. It will make these geysers seem like bubbles bursting in a pond."

Bren watched the birds soaring with the spray, calling out their morning songs. He turned to go, but Josk said, "Even the birds will be flung into the void."

Bren hurried toward the kitchen. He had no time for Josk's rantings. Quakes had killed hundreds of people during the past year, but you couldn't allow yourself to be paralyzed. If the world blew apart and they all became cinders in space, so be it.

Yet he knew Josk was quoting the sages and prophets. The planet was unstable. Millennia ago, according to their own Askirit beliefs, the Maker had judged the world. It had been rent by a cataclysmic collision, with great hollows opened in the darkness below. The only people who had survived were those who had fallen deep beneath the seared skin of the planet.

In that night world, the survivors had formed alliances and cultures, learning to live in the darkness, sustained by the richness of the waters that daily poured down into subterranean oceans.

Only in the past century had anyone found the way up. The Maker had sent his own to lead them up to the light and to heal their eyes when they emerged. Decades later, a blind princess named Mela had gone back down to show others the way out.

Once again, the Maker had sent his own, rescuing many, and Mela had become queen.

Bren, partly of barbarian stock, was her humble soldier. He wanted nothing more than to prove himself loyal to Mela, to the Askirit religion, to the future of their troubled kingdom. And that meant pleasing his difficult captain, who had ordered him to fetch the commander's breakfast.

A stocky, middle-aged woman glared at Bren as he entered the cold kitchen. She had just lighted the fire and was holding slivers of kindling against the little flame. "I suppose you're not here to help, just to get something." She said nothing more until she finally succeeded in getting some split logs burning. She then turned toward him. "No one's here to help me today, so don't expect much."

His heart sank. He knew his captain would berate him for not getting a decent breakfast to his commander on time. But what was he to do? He felt like such an outsider in the Royal House that even the cook intimidated him.

"I'm here for the commander's breakfast."

With one hand the woman pulled from her forehead strands of thin strawberry-blonde hair and with the other dug out utensils from the triangular storage area. "You can have it cold or cooked. Cooked takes time." Her face was full of creases, the deepest ones turned down at the corners of her mouth. "With no help, I can barely get breakfast for the royals."

He shrugged with his palms open toward her. "I'll help."

She thrust a knife, cutting board, and bread at him, then rushed to feed the fire again.

Bren happened to be looking at the cook's face when a visitor entered behind him. The weary creases suddenly lifted into a large smile. "Welcome, Gresen." He turned to see a thin old woman carrying a large bundle in a blanket.

The cook, making cooing sounds, rushed to the woman and pulled back a corner of the blanket. Bren saw a bit of tiny cheek under her thick hand.

He grimaced. That was all he needed—a baby slowing the cook down. He sliced bread hurriedly, as if to send them a message, but they casually laid the baby on the table, pulling the blankets away.

"Meleden." Had he heard right? Yes, the cook was calling the baby Meleden. The name jarred him, for Meleden was the queen's infant daughter who had caused so much turmoil.

He glanced nervously at the women. He well remembered the proclamations nearly two years before. After bearing many sons, Queen Mela had birthed a daughter. She had named her Meleden, as her own namesake and after her husband's sister, Delas. Meleden, "the Maker's blessing."

But after the feasting and festivities, word trickled out that Meleden was not a blessing after all. She was deaf and blind. Gossips whispered she had no more mind than a cabbage.

Finally came a terse royal announcement. The infant daughter was not well and might die.

The news had slashed through the nation. Those who hated Askirit rule said that judgment had visited the Royal House and that Mela's reign was doomed. The military was put on alert. Bren, who fiercely believed in Mela's reign, had joined up.

The women seemed fastened to the bundle on the table. "Fire's dying," he said, hoping to stir them.

"Thank you," the cook said, as if he'd offered to tend it. Reluctantly he added logs and stirred the flames. He hated his timidity.

"What's next?" he demanded.

The thin old nurse motioned him over.

He shook his head no, but she locked on him a gaze as severe as the white streaks in her black hair. They reminded him of military slashes. He moved toward her.

Gresen tucked a folded little blanket under the infant's head. "Look at her."

The girl's wide, soft face astounded him. She was large—nearly two years old—yet like a newborn breath from another world. Just a sleeping baby, but somehow she brought into his senses mysterious music he found himself straining to hear.

"Touch her."

His hand, poised above her lips, slowly, slowly floated down and grazed the little royal cheek. The contact rippled through him.

Her old nurse stared into Bren's eyes, appraising. "Some are drawn to Meleden. Others flee the glory."

The cook said, "We have known all the queen's children. None have shaken her with such grief. Yet none have given her so much love."

He could not understand that. "Does she respond at all?"

"Rarely a smile. Rarely a response of any kind."

Gresen's eyes were still locked on his, but they broke away at the voices of children racing in the corridors. She calmly lifted Meleden and, before Bren could object, had placed her into his arms. "My other charges need a firm word." She motioned the cook to come with her and was gone before he could stop her.

Bren found himself standing awkwardly with the warm bundle, wondering how to position her head. His immediate thought was of his captain walking in and finding him like this, the commander's breakfast not even started. What if the baby spat up all over the uniform he was forever fussing with?

These were his thoughts, but not his feelings. Strangely, his timidity was ebbing. Holding her was like drawing close to a fire's warmth. No, it was more like being surrounded by warmth, by warm presences soaking life into his bones.

Meleden felt limp and weighty. Two-year-olds, he thought, weren't meant to be bundled in blankets. They should run and climb, flitting from one thing to another; but she lay against his chest like a newborn.

Behind him he sensed someone had re-entered the room. He was now reluctant to give her up and didn't turn but stood holding Meleden for a moment. Then he turned to give her back to the women, but no one was there.

Yet someone was in the room. From the doorway someone was radiating the same warmth he felt from the child.

It lasted only a few moments, until the women briskly walked back in. They found him staring vacantly.

Gresen held out her arms for the baby. "Everything all right?"

He slowly surrendered her. "Yes."

She placed the child back on the table, and as she made her head comfortable, Meleden opened her eyes. Bren was bent over, studying her. "What does she see?"

"More than we do." Gresen said it with such instant certitude Bren's eyes snapped up to catch her expression. Her smile and crinkled eyes were equally certain. "The sages have said all through the centuries that the babe in the womb learns mysteries that would astound us. Each beat of the child's heart nurtures new wisdom."

Bren nodded. "But the birth cries, they say, start the forgetting . . . and only later, when we least expect it, do we feel the inexpressible longings."

Gresen waved her fingers before the infant's eyes but got no response. "Meleden, you're still being born. So precious to the Maker you're still becoming what we cannot imagine."

Bren watched the child's open, unseeing eyes. Such a beautiful little girl, yet unable to do anything but swallow and cry. Why was she born? And what had he sensed in the room with him?

The cook was finally chopping at a thick ham, shoving pieces into a skillet. She motioned to Bren to place it over the fire. "You've heard that little Meleden is a curse on this house. But we know—and you know—that the child is a gift."

Gresen cradled the baby in her arms. "Her mother also knows it. She cannot hold Meleden without weeping. She calls her the 'Morning Child.' The promise of the morning to come."

The Quake

The captain glared at several platoons standing at attention. He had requested volunteers to spy out the mountains and city of their increasingly powerful enemies, the Mazcaens.

No one had spoken. Everyone knew what the Mazcaens did to captives.

Bren had never, ever volunteered for anything. If the captain had asked for a volunteer to take a walk on the royal lawn, Bren would have remained silent. He looked at the ground, shutting out sight of the angry officer, still relieved that the lateness of the commander's breakfast had not caused him trouble.

His father had been timid, and Bren figured he had inherited his timidity from him. A simple tanner of unrelenting industry and loyalty, his father feared upsetting anyone. Born a barbarian, he worried that he was mistrusted.

In contrast, his mother was born Askirit and moved like a lioness among cubs. Bren had none of her sense of station and presence. He inherited his father's pain in the gut, the desire to please above all else, the anxiety that he might fail and be humiliated.

That's why he astounded himself when he raised his eyes to the captain. Bren's father was not only barbarian but part Mazcaen. He felt compelled to volunteer. Clenching his hands, he forced the words past his lips. "I volunteer to go, Sir."

He had been able to say it only by concentrating on the face of the infant princess. In those moments in the kitchen, he had found some courage. Perhaps more important, he had gained the conviction that his fierce desire to serve the kingdom must not be smothered by cowardice.

Yet it was only a little courage. As the captain stalked up to him and gave him his orders, he could barely get out the appropriate responses. When two other soldiers were ordered to go with him, he groaned inside. They would hate him for volunteering, hate his leading them, hate being the ones ordered to go. He imagined ahead of him one humiliating failure after another.

In reality, Bren's first venture in leadership involved no humiliations at all. The two men with him, Kemm and Treskin, hated the mission but feared capture. They readily let Bren take the point, knowing he had Mazcaen blood and hoping he understood them.

Until recently, being Mazcaen hadn't meant much. They were just one of many pagan tribes the Askirit felt superior to. But Belez, the Mazcaen city in the mountains, was growing stronger and stronger. A day's hard march away, it sent increasing numbers of deadly raiding parties against the Askirit villages by the sea. Bren knew the myths by which Belez was built, knew how the leaders gained power, knew the language and lore. Since its rising, he hated his Mazcaen blood and was ready to do anything to atone for it.

The three had scouted trails leading into Belez, watched the commerce and military movements. Every crunch of leaves and twigs under their boots thrust into their minds images of Mazcaen tortures. But now they had returned to a familiar ridge not far from the royal grounds of Kelerai and the tension was gone from their faces.

Yet even here Bren couldn't get away from his anxious intensity. He hated logistics. As they stripped off their sweaty packs to make camp, he worried about picking the proper spot, remembering the warnings about drainage and his instructor's booming admonition, "You want to wake up in puddles? Even on a hill, water collects just where it's nice and flat."

As the others made a fire, he climbed a higher ridge to reconnoiter. A big burr oak stood at a high point, and he climbed it to look at the Royal House in the distance.

The king who had preceded Mela had reigned from an elaborate palace in Aris, the proud capital city ever since their people had first emerged from the darkness generations ago. Aris had been named and patterned after their ancestors' capital deep in the planet. But when Mela had become queen, she had given the palace in Aris to the unfortunate. She chose as the nation's new capital the little tourist haven named for the great geysers. The city of Kelerai was far inland from Aris, but its grand phenomenon symbolized pristine power; she wanted the Askirit to constantly rise to its grandeur.

Yet she also embraced simplicity. She had made her old school in Kelerai the Royal House. Mela's father had warned her that it was unfit for the queen, that the ramshackle structures were too close to kelerai and might one day be shattered. She had insisted it was perfect for the royal family to be drenched and shaken and exhilarated by kelerai every day, and that the queen—of all people—should stand at the edge of the world's instability.

But the old king's relatives seethed, hating the fact that by Mela's saving the nation, they had been cast aside.

Bren loved all the stories about Mela's courage and faith and whispered many vows of loyalty as he sat looking at the royal house and, to his right, the growing city of Kelerai that had become the nation's new capital.

The tree shifted under him.

Before his mind could grab at what was going on, it moved again. And again and again, like a giant under him bending his knees and swaying back and forth.

The ground at the tree's base split, ripping away part of the trunk and some branches, which toppled into the crevasse and disappeared. Bren's hands clamped on the thick branch under him. The crevasse opened, closed, opened again. The tree lifted, turned and tilted, then he felt it sliding down.

Bren pulled his clamped hands loose and scrambled upward for higher branches, but the tree was toppling and almost horizontal. He kept getting jerked back and forth, not knowing where to find solid ground. He tried to brace himself so he could leap away, but the tree gave a mighty lurch and suddenly he was plunging straight down amid entangling branches.

A jarring impact reverberated from his feet up through his body just before everything in front of him and behind him rushed together and ground dirt and rocks against his body. Colors exploded in his mind as pain radiated through his chest. He tried to gasp for air but not even his lungs moved.

He felt warm. A calmness coursed through him, and he felt released from his imprisonment, released into pure air. He was moving upward faster and faster. He felt light was wrapped around him, churning around him and in him and lifting him so that when he looked down he saw the mountains below. From along the ragged pattern of the quake cutting through mountains and valleys, streaks and wavering bands of light were rising, scores of them. They seemed to be persons like himself, some racing past him and going higher, others steadily floating up.

Two persons were beside him, talking to him, persons more than twice his size, all wrapped in light as he was, their faces brighter than their bodies. He seemed to be no longer rising; these shining ones were walking and he longed to walk forever with them.

He felt welcomed. He felt known. He felt they knew everything about him and that he was let in on the joke. Let in on all the jokes. Their thoughts were crackling with humor, their words laced with a wise merriment that put everything wonderfully right.

They were even full of humor about his going back, that they would have to stuff him into that little body down there and he would hardly fit but they could do the job if he'd stop chuckling so much.

Bren didn't want to go back. What was this about going back? Above he saw a grassy place with a warm green light behind it and figures entering, and he wanted to go to them. But the celestials said they would bend him in all the right places to get him back into himself, and he felt the light all around him fading.

The Royal Family

Bren was trying to find the shining ones, trying to speak to them. Suddenly his voice surprised him by breaking painfully out of his throat and reaching his ears like an alien croak.

"What?" Breathing came close to his face. "Bren?"

He didn't want to repeat the pain in his throat so he opened his eyes. Treskin's blurred mouth above him was moving, saying something about the quake. "Ripped through the Royal House and half the city."

Bren lifted his head and looked around. Bodies lay on the grass like bundles of dirty clothing.

"Are they all dead?" The pain of talking radiated from his throat into his jaw.

"These were all breathing when we brought them." Soldiers fumbling with water bottles and medical bags moved around them in a noisy chaos. Someone shouted Treskin's name. He put water by Bren's head and left.

Despite his pain and his dismay at the carnage, the deep reservoir of peace remained. He even felt the humor from the celestial ones bubbling up inside, making him want to smile though there was nothing to smile about.

But, he thought, there is something to smile about. He was still knowing, from above the mountains, that all things converge into the holy purposes that bring holy laughter to all creation. His experience had changed everything. He was breathing changed air, hearing with different ears, seeing what those men of light saw.

He lay listening to the moans around him, yet his fears were gone. He sensed he had nothing to fear. He had been brought back, and deep tragedy could come only if he fought against his own mission, fought against his own determination to walk in the light.

Treskin was beside him again, leaning over, offering him water. He told of their seeing a strip of Bren's red shirt on a branch sticking up from the crevasse, of how they'd found him wedged among thick branches mostly buried but, oddly, his face free. None of it seemed important. Instead, as Treskin talked, Bren thought about how he had resented him and other Askirit companions for not having to carry the burden of Mazcaen blood. He remembered how often he had nursed self-pity, in contrast to his new otherworldly love for Treskin and for everyone tending the barely surviving and the dying.

He saw through the eyes of the celestials, the same ones, he was convinced, who had stood in the kitchen with him and the infant princess.

Treskin described the devastation, looking haggard as he told Bren the worst: that every one of the royal family had been killed.

For Bren, it meant the end of everything. Those who had whispered that the birth of Meleden was an ill omen would cackle now that the queen's house had been destroyed. He realized now why the soldiers around him tending the dead and dying on the bloody grass seemed themselves so lifeless.

But Bren had seen all those flares of light speeding below him and then upward, souls bolting home. He smiled, thinking of Mela and her children surely among them.

With great effort he said, "They are not dead, you know."

Treskin's head nodded absently. "That is the hope," he said, but his voice had no hope in it.

"I've seen them!" Bren said. "They're alive."

Treskin ignored the words. He spoke instead of Mazcaen raids beginning already along the coast; the kingdom was disintegrating. Their enemies would brutally seize the moment. He was not greatly interested in conjectures about the ultimate fate of the royal family.

Old Festik

Bren regained strength remarkably fast; even the pain receded after several days. But other than his one comment to Treskin, he said nothing about his experiences while buried in the rubble. He simply relived it into his senses again and again and spread hope wherever he could.

Yet the buoyancy and fearlessness were slowly fading, so that he had to keep reminding himself of what he had experienced. He felt enormously changed and was still filled with amazement. Yet again and again he purposely had to turn his emotions and his will toward that light which he had both seen and felt, for he felt other forces constantly pulling him away from it.

He carried food to the living, and because the leaders felt hope in him that they did not have themselves, they often called him to pray with the dying. He was on his knees beside a man who moments before had ceased breathing when he felt a presence behind him. He looked up; a black-robed woman was bending to sit beside him.

He assumed the woman was a relative. "He's dead." Bren reached over and closed the man's mouth.

"I know."

"He is now more alive than you or I."

"I know that too." The woman pulled away her covering and revealed her face; it was Gresen. She hushed his greeting with a little shake of the head.

"I thought you were dead," he whispered. "All the royal family, all the guards . . ."

"They're all dead. I was in the far garden, knocked flat."

He reached over and grasped her old hand with both of his. "You too were family."

She shuddered. "How could anyone have ever thought that Mela, the blessed of the Maker, the one who had served him so magnificently, should be destroyed and be made into a proverb of doom?"

He shook his head. "That's only this wicked world's judgment."

Bren motioned to a passing soldier that the man at his knees had died. Then he walked with Gresen out of the camp.

"I'm told they found the bodies of the royal family."

She nodded. "I stood at a distance and watched them work in the rubble. Watched them recover every one."

"Except the baby? Someone said no one found the baby."

"She didn't need to be found."

He looked at her sharply, wondering if he might see a little smile, might see a sign the baby was still alive. But her lips were pursed tightly.

"I had her in my arms, watching them dig. She came though the quake without a whimper." The old woman grimaced, and her eyes took on a steely look. "I was so bowed with grief that I never heard old Festik coming. He ripped her out of my arms!"

Bren had never heard of old Festik. Gresen told him he was a drunk who prowled the grounds, always begging money. "But what would he do with a baby?" Bren asked. "A baby everyone knows and no one would want?"

She hushed him again. "That's why we've been whispering. I don't want anyone to know Festik took Meleden. They'd know there's only one way for him to get money for her—from the Mazcaens." Her lower jaw had started trembling a little, and she pressed her palm against her chin. "It would have been much, much better if she and I had both died in the quake."

Bren found the captain among rows of tents filled with convalescents, talking in a high, nervous voice to three subordinates. One said something about being wide open to attack.

Previously, Bren would never have approached his captain, even in the best of times. But now he was sensing his fears, heedless of his own anxieties. He asked to have a word with him, and eventually the captain led him to the edge of a stream.

"Only days ago, you sent me to spy on the Mazcaens. But now there's a far more urgent matter." The captain's eyes kept moving, studying Bren's face for an instant, like a hummingbird at a flower, then darting elsewhere to look for movements in the distance. Bren sensed it didn't matter how the captain responded to him, only that he keep his own determination. "I'm willing to go again."

The captain frowned. "We need every man right here. An attack may come any minute." He spoke sharply, as if this conversation was a waste of his time.

"If an attack comes, I won't make any difference. But if it doesn't, what I find out could change everything."

The captain raised high his eyebrows and appraised Bren. He was not in a mood to argue with a common soldier.

"I'd go alone, I'd enter Belez alone. That's the only way to learn what the enemy is planning."

This last made the captain's face tighten in amazement. "You'll writhe and dance for them—after they paint you!" He was studying Bren as if to decipher him.

"Maybe. But if I come back, you'll find out what's coming at us."

The captain's eyes tightened. Bren found it odd that they had so thoroughly switched roles, the officer fretting and anxious, yet in relative safety, Bren calm and determined to walk into the enemy's stronghold. The captain studied him for a long time, then finally agreed.

"I'm fully loyal," Bren assured him. "I have Mazcaen blood in me, but I'm half Askirit. Passionately Askirit! I'd never betray you."

The captain produced his first smile. "They wouldn't have any use for you. Not a soldier of the queen. They'd far rather use you to spark up a ceremony."

Bren's pack was bulging as he pulled it off his back and settled against an old pine. He had come to watch the eruption of kelerai.

The scar from the deadly quake was barely discernible, a thin rift running through the crumpled Royal House, parallel to where the geysers would burst in the distance.

He had agreed to meet Gresen here before setting out. He spied her coming up the trail leading a weathered old donkey. When she reached him, he stood and raised his eyebrows quizzically.

In answer to his look she said, "I'm off to Aris." She tied the rope to a branch and let the donkey graze.

Bren had heard that the queen's distant relatives and the relatives of the previous king were all insisting the capital be moved back to Aris. "So Queen Mela gave the King's House there to the maimed and crippled, and now they've been thrown out?"

"They have." She sat down and he settled beside her. "I spoke to a blind man who came back from there." She wrinkled her nose in disgust. "He says the royals—every relative the old king or Queen Mela ever had—are rooting around in the house talking about who should rule. But they're all terrified of what the Mazcaens do to kings!" She laughed without mirth. "So they mill around in the King's House. The old king's relatives say Mela was judged; hers say

Mela saved the kingdom. But it doesn't matter. None of them would dare become king or queen anyway."

"So who *will* rule?"

Gresen put her fist in the air. "I wish Varial would become queen. The Enre could lead us!"

Bren nodded. The Enre were a fiercely religious order of Askirit women, uniquely trained in their own martial arts. From times of their ancestors in the darkness of Aliare beneath them, Varial was the name of the Enre's appointed leader. The current Varial had been appointed only a year before.

The old woman slowly lowered her fist. "But Varial says it's not her time."

Kelerai began its rumblings; they turned their eyes toward it. Gresen told Bren she was going to Aris because she might be needed to tend royal children there. "No one here needs me."

Kelerai erupted and they stared in silent wonder. Bren said, "It's even higher now, don't you think?"

"I doubt it. After every quake people say that, but it never seems so to me."

"Yet the ground shakes more. I get the feeling Josk is right. Sometime kelerai is going to split this old world apart."

As they felt kelerai's spray and heard the birds soaring and singing with it, Bren found himself telling her everything about his own soaring with the creatures of light. "It changed everything in me. When I first came to, I saw sparkles of light in Treskin's beard. I saw the sparkling in the trees, the grass, even my boots. I still see it—I can see it in your face. But not as bright as when I first awoke."

He told her the celestials had sent him back. "I feel the way I did with Meleden, the same peace and energy."

As Gresen had listened, her manner had completely changed. He had not seen her so peaceful since the morning she had put Meleden into his arms. "The infant is an omen come into the world, unexpected, uncomprehended." She put her thin hand on his neck. "And now, so are you."

Chapter 2.

—— The Welcome Catastrophe ——

Laren was not a slave. That would have been far too much for her to hope for.

Slaves got beaten at times, but they didn't worry constantly about finding a handful of corn or a place to huddle through the night in the cold. If she were a slave, at least someone would want her to survive. Laren was a canyon's depth beneath the lowest slave.

She was an Ishtel.

The young woman was at the river picking up the clothing she had washed and had spread out to dry, enormously grateful that her work might lead to a little food. She barely heard the shouts above her on the walkways of the city of Belez.

The sounds grew louder and finally she looked up. Four young Mazcaen soldiers stood on a balcony jutting out above the grassy descent to the river. "Dead! All of them!" they jubilantly shouted down. She stood and looked up uncomprehending, and as she did so, they saw by her golden hair and white skin that she was an Ishtel.

Instantly they turned and took their news in another direction.

She picked up the clothing she had so carefully washed, holding it like a tray of precious gems. They were garments of the royal children, garments Laren could never have hoped to even see, let alone touch. But Galial, a slave in the royal household, had been kind to her and had given her this little task. The enormous trust Galial had placed in her made her gait slow and awkward, as if she were about to drop her frightening cargo.

She chose the city walkway at the lowest level, anxious to be inconspicuous. She passed symbolic images on every wall and imbedded in each cause way. They all celebrated the myth of the kingdom's founder, Mazc, which was chanted in every ceremony within the city's walls:

A hurricane struck a village.
Mazc was flung into the air.
He struck a tree, and his hands clamped down.
The winds wanted him;
The winds tore at him and lifted his body,
But his hands tethered him to the ground.
The winds failed; Mazc looked at his hands.
They gripped a shattered tent pole,
Driven into the heart of the tree.
From its end flapped a pennant of tent cloth.
Mazc ripped the pole free and held it high,
Shouting his challenge to the winds.

The Mazcaens told many such tales. How Mazc, shattered pole in hand, had seen in the mountain's peak above him a formation of swirling stone identical to the flapping pennant. How under that peak he had founded a kingdom based on martial energy— bringing order and discipline into the world's chaos.

Laren was walking past a great mural depicting king after king marching toward the temple, each holding aloft a shattered pole and pennant. All the walkways led to the temple and its surrounding buildings; every wall was carved and painted with symbols of a fist holding a flapping pennant.

Laren did not look at the gigantic kings as she walked past them, nor did she look up at the mountain peak in which the Mazcaens believed they saw the shapes of their holy pennant. They meant nothing to her; she concentrated on keeping her eyes lowered but keeping alert.

When she saw a man dressed as a slave walking in her direction, she crossed out of the way. Brushing against any man could bring an angry roar or a hail of blows. Slaves were often the worst. Some said in their luckless lives they had only one happiness—to strike out at clumsy Ishtels.

Inside the squat building farthest from the temple, wide stone stairs led to rooms below the royal residences. She stuck her head into the one in which clothing was cleaned and stored but saw only neat piles. Quickly she stepped away; someone finding her alone in the room would assume she was there to steal.

From the scullery down the hall she heard Galial's voice. This was a hopeful sign; very hopeful. The scullery was connected to the granary with its bins of grains. Galial might be able to slip her a little sack of corn or rice. She had eaten nothing since yesterday.

She came to the doorway's edge, trying to see Galial so she could walk directly to her. She didn't want to have someone else see her first and yell at her to get out.

Laren spied Galial among several women scouring and storing pots and was just about to move toward her when a pair of legs and big shoulders burst through the doorway. She was tilted slightly off balance as the big male body stumbled by her, grazing her shoulder.

Laren blanched. She had tried to stay out of the way, intent on locating Galial, only her head poked into the doorway. She had never heard him coming. Her throat constricted as she tensed for his harsh words and likely a slap across her face.

But the man ignored her. "The quake!" he declared, and everyone turned toward him. They had felt the distant rumblings the day before and all had talked about it. "Ripped right through

Kelerai," he said with contagious excitement. "Ripped right through the Askirit Royal House!"

The young man was a slave about her age. He spoke with inordinate pride, as if delivering this momentous declaration was the most weighty deed he might ever perform.

The slaves' faces had become like bobbing sunflowers, soaking up his words like bright rays, as if this good news for their masters was just as much theirs. When the young man had told all he knew, they shook their heads in wonder and kept talking about it as they turned back to washing utensils.

The young man noticed Laren just inside the doorway. For the slightest instant, before she could drop her gaze, their eyes locked. "The royal family is dead. All of them," he declared, lips pursed, jaw jutted out in satisfaction. "The queen and every prince."

No man but an Ishtel had ever before spoken to Laren. She stepped further back against the wall, but he merely bolted past her to carry the news elsewhere.

She found Galial and gave her the washed clothes. The older woman barely nodded. When Laren asked for a little corn, she merely pointed to the vast bin, the slave woman's eyes still darting from face to face as they spoke of hundreds killed and the collapse of their enemy and the ascending greatness of the Mazcaen kingdom.

The Red-Haired Child

Captives from raids, roped together and hunched low, were filing into buildings on the far side of the temple as Laren hurried on. She had no thoughts about them, barely glancing in their direction as she clutched her pile of washed clothing. Her mind was on her stomach, for her corn was gone and she didn't know if this time she would be given food for her work. Even captives were

more important than she was, for they were at least worth sacrific-
ing. To consecrate a building, captives would be killed and buried
in its foundation, their blood and bodies part of the great rituals of
the city. But an Ishtel's blood and body could only pollute.

Laren had barely entered the room when Galial urgently
motioned her closer. Obviously upset, the big woman hurriedly
stacked into Laren's arms three baskets of clothes. She could barely
see over them and she wondered if Galial had gotten a harsh command with dire threats. Slaves too were sacrificed in temple rituals.

Galial precariously balanced two tall stacks of baskets in her
own arms and started down the hall. Laren followed her bulky
form, worried as they started up a flight of stairs that she would
drop a basket or that Galial might fall back on her.

They were soon in a great room with countless rows of pre-
cisely divided shelves reaching to the ceiling, a royal bird's head
insignia on each section. Carefully, Galial squatted and eased her
baskets onto the floor.

This level was only a half-flight below the royal residences.
Laren had never been this high before; to be even in the work areas
below was unusual and intimidating for an Ishtel. Colors she had
never seen before were folded into so many shapes she could not
comprehend it all. Every garment had a mystical quality, for they
were worn and touched and made remarkable by those infinitely
above her.

Galial gasped. Laren jerked her head toward her, then to the
doorway. Standing there was a girl of about twelve with bright red
hair in a silver and blue smock. She wore a wide headband with an
ornate, soft clump of bright feathers on the side.

"We're unloading the baskets," Galial said, her hands digging
into one, her fearful voice more obsequious than even Laren's had
ever been. The distance from Laren to this privileged child was so
vast as to defy her thoughts.

The girl was paying no attention to Galial. She was looking
intently at Laren, who had turned halfway toward her, still holding the baskets. "Who's this?" The child's voice was shrill.

"She just helped me carry the baskets up." Galial's voice was an agony of fear.

The girl stepped close to Laren, who was peering just over the top of a green blanket on top of the highest basket. The royal child held an intricately carved white stick; she used it to push the basket aside to reveal Laren's face. "You're an Ishtel!" she accused.

Laren managed to keep the basket from falling even as she lowered her eyes. But she had seen the child's face, rather plain contrasted with her striking red hair and splendid clothes. The royal little girl looked shocked yet intrigued, like someone who had found in her room a giant cockroach with a human face.

Staring at the floor, bending her knees slightly, Laren tried to squat as Galial had in order to put down the baskets. "Who told you to move?" The girl's stick whacked against the top basket, knocking it to the floor. Laren stood erect again; the child walked closer, stood for a long time studying her. A head shorter, she put the end of her stick on Laren's chin and poked upward. "Get your eyes off the floor!"

Slowly Laren raised her eyes, not knowing where to focus them. She looked off in Galial's direction, but the stick rapped her jaw so that she was forced to face the girl. Instantly the girl locked her eyes on Laren's, as if to penetrate distasteful, alien secrets. The child's lips were full and thickly rounded, her nose wide, her skin reddish brown, darker than Galial's. Skin red and rich as loam and precious stones, Laren had always been told.

"Put down the baskets." Laren eased them down, then stood again, looking above the girl to avoid her eyes. She felt the child's stick hook itself in a ragged gap in her thin dress. She felt the fabric tear as the stick ripped it open to expose her pale arm and shoulder. "White as a peeled beech," the girl said. "White as a maggot in rat meat."

The child took another step closer and reached up to touch her face. Laren was surprised that her fingers were trembling as they traced across her thin lips and narrow features. But she was not surprised when the little fingers grasped her nose and wrenched it painfully with her thumb and forefingers, for that was the mark of disgust used on Ishtels. The custom had started in the darkness below when Ishtels had first been made lower than slaves—a rough twist, then spitting out the word "lice-eater." The phrase referred to a slimy carrion beetle with long feelers and a bristly tail.

The little girl mouthed "lice-eater" with as much disgust as Laren had ever heard from slave lips. Then she whipped her stick across Laren's face. The blow struck her on cheekbone and temple, flinging stars into her mind and pain across her face. Then she felt the stick strike the other side of her face, and she struggled to stand steady. Her eyes sought the floor, crossing over the girl's expression. The regal, curved lips were tightly bunched together, as if deliberating on the proper thing to do with this oddity.

The dark little girl looked down at her white stick; it was streaked with glistening red on one edge. "Blood! You've gotten lice-eater blood on my stick!" Her hands shook. She looked back and forth from Galial to Laren. Suddenly she walked over to Galial and struck her also, right across the face. "You brought that blood up here!"

The red-haired girl then turned and stormed out of the room.

Through her own pain Laren saw the red welt rise from Galial's lower cheek to her forehead. The big woman stood like a stone, but her eyes were full of tears.

Laren had no tears, just dry terror.

Galial's bosom heaved in a great sigh, and Laren was almost ready to run to her as she had years before when her mother was alive, run to her and bury herself within the ample folds of her dress. But Galial's words came out as savage as a mastiff's growl: "Get out! Get out of here!"

——— Earthworms ———

Laren found a half-eaten piece of melon and eagerly chewed into it. She was used to the stench of the garbage field, but she hated smelling like it herself. After coming here to scavenge, unlike many Ishtels she would go straight to the river to wash.

"Lots of meat on these bones." She looked up to see Cenek, an Ishtel her age, holding three long ribs in his hand. He took a determined bite at the gristle on one end, and Laren wiped the juice from her own mouth when she saw the grease on his. With a familiar sing-song slur he said, "Come on over here, Worm."

She moved toward him, rind in hand. She didn't mind being called "Worm"—Ishtels ruefully used the word for themselves, finding it far less repugnant than the names the Mazcaens used. Earthworms were ordinary things. Digging in a garden, one wasn't repulsed by slicing one in half. Stitching a wriggling worm on a hook was a necessary part of fishing. Ishtels were somehow necessary also.

"What happened to your face?" Cenek asked.

"Nothing much."

"Two welts like that, one on each side? Somebody did it to you."

Laren knew she'd end up telling him, though she didn't want him to know about her little jobs and the catastrophe that had ruined it all. But nothing interested Ishtels more than injuries, for they were anxious to avoid what had happened to someone else. She told him the whole story.

His eyes bored into hers, questioning this preposterous story of actually being spoken to by a royal child just a half-floor beneath the royal rooms. He cocked his head and scrunched up his face. "I never go anywhere near there." He told her his most recent brush with authorities was being shouted aside by soldiers surrounding something as they were rushing toward the temple complex. "Must have been the royal baby they stole from the Askirit."

Her mind was still on her own experiences; his changing the subject annoyed her. "What baby? I thought all the enemy royals were killed."

He offered her a corn cob with a few kernels still attached at one end. She bit off all the kernels and started chewing on the cob.

"This one must have been somewhere else. But no difference. They'll probably sacrifice it in one of those all-night ceremonies."

Laren was not interested. Her eyes, always searching for clothing, had spied a scrap of red cloth poking out from a pile of bones and husks. She walked over to it and yanked it free but found it was only a torn sleeve. She kicked around at the debris but found no more of the garment.

"Found a cap a few days ago," he said. "Perfectly good except it had been here so long."

She wrinkled her nose. She was glad he wasn't wearing the cap. Anything in these heaps even a little while had to be scrubbed and soaked for days to lose the odor. Cenek, dressed in layers of torn and mismatched strips and pieces, smelled like the heaps themselves.

He located more corn, and as he offered her another cob with two bands of kernels, he sidled close to her. He was always wanting to touch her, but she stepped back as she accepted the corn.

"You have beautiful eyes." She knew what he meant by the cliché. He wanted to hold her, but he saw no beauty in her. Everyone knew the thin lips and narrow faces of Ishtels were ugly and undesirable.

She said thank you, but she meant that she knew young men talked about "beautiful eyes" only when they wanted a girl. She often wondered what it had been like between her mother and father. The Ishtels had no marriage—that was for slaves and their masters. Yet her mother had been faithful to her father. He had died when she was a little girl, and she remembered the sadness.

But when her mother had more recently died, it had been more than a loss. Laren had been deserted, a nestling bird fallen on hard, cold ground. No one cared if she starved or froze. No one brought her warmth. The only one now who wanted to hold her was Cenek.

Once she had felt glimmers of warmth from Galial. That was gone now; she could never return.

Cenek put his hand on her shoulder. He too had no obligations, only desires. She gently pushed away from him, making a light comment. Though she still felt very hungry, she left for the river. Yet she wondered why she should bother to wash away the stench any more. Why do anything but scavenge and stay out of people's way?

The Lower Vaults

Outside the city, on gray loose stone that butted against a steep rise, Laren sat opposite an Ishtel man named Kol. He was gaunt, middle-aged, but with the deep facial furrows and slow movements of an old man. Ishtels, it was said, never lived long enough to see their grandchildren.

Kol was making music, such as it was, with stones in each hand clacking at the end of each woeful phrase he uttered. His eyes were closed, as if his hands were being tortured by his dexterous clacking of the stones in them. At his saddest words, he would crash both hands together, the dull noise echoing lifeless as his laments. When Ishtels weren't scavenging, they were making a sort of sad music in their hands with stones or rocks or shells, sometimes humming or singing woeful songs, but usually just clicking or snapping or grinding.

Laren had sandstone in her own hands, thudding them together with his rhythm, letting the sand trickle through her fingers until only little bits were left gritty against her palms.

Sometimes Kol told her stories her ancestors had shared in the darkness below, stories of remarkable heroism. But the valiant were never Ishtels. In fact, her people never had any role in the stories at all. Royal princes and great ones fought fearsome beasts and hostile tribes. They founded kingdoms. But the Ishtels were no more part of that than were carrion beetles.

She had heard an old slave once say, "Ishtels are grease on a winch. When you smear rancid fat on the ropes, you hate the smell; you hate the feel of the grease on your hands. But it's necessary.

You smear it on, and you ignore the smell." The slave had laughed.
"Ishtels are grease." She had heard him say those words as she
scavenged on her knees in a harvested field, picking at the stray
grains, stuffing whatever she found directly into her mouth.

Hunched against the breeze, ruthlessly crushing chunks of
sandstone in her hands, Laren told Kol what the slave had said.

"Well, at least grease is needed." His jaw jutted out, trembling a little like his hands. "They need someone to spit at." He spit
into the rocks himself, then brightened a little, as if he were about
to share something good. "It's true they can strike us whenever
they want. They can kill us or drive us into the desert. But remember this: they won't ever slaughter all of us. We're needed. The
slave was right."

She barely listened as he described this thin scrap of dignity.
The little dreams instilled by her mother were gone. She dusted
her hands of the crushed sandstone, picked up some hard pebbles
and absently clicked them together.

With big rocks in each hand, Kol was making a steady klunk,
klunk, klunk. "Even if Ishtels aren't needed," he said, as if he had
been reevaluating the slave's assertion, "even if no one needs us,
we're wily. Wary and wily. They'll never break us all."

She stared at the bleak rockscape, grinding more sandstone
against the pebbles till they rolled in a residue of lumpy granules.

"Laren!" The voice rang with authority, a sound never heard
here where Ishtels slept. She looked up and saw Galial standing at
a distance, hand outstretched, index finger beckoning her to come.

A moment before, Laren had felt inert as a rock; now she
quivered like an alert deer. If the king himself had appeared, she
would have been no more dumbfounded. Laren scrambled toward
her, wondering at her extraordinary visit.

The big woman stood like a statue. A slight smile creased her
face, letting out a trace of the warmth Laren so longed for. Yet as
Laren drew near, she also wrinkled her nose. "Go and wash. Then
come to me at noon."

Galial turned as smartly as a soldier and walked away, leaving the young woman amazed and energized by this fleshy apparition.

When Laren appeared at noon, Galial didn't hand her an armload of dirty clothes. Instead, she marched the scrubbed young woman down yet another level, telling her that three women were sick and that she would be put to work.

Infrequent candles gave barely enough wavering light to maneuver down the corridor. She reached out and touched the cold stone; she had never been so deep beneath the surface. A guard with a stubby double-bladed ax and a short sword in his belt barked out a challenge. Galial held out a carved identification seal, and as he let them pass, he made the sarcastic sniffing sound that meant he smelled an Ishtel.

At the corridor's end, six guards blocked their way. Galial presented the stone seal; they parted so the women could enter.

Despite the many candles burning in the large rock-hewn chamber, Laren had to squint to make out the low shapes in the far corner. A woman was bending over a little bed, gently wiping something. Then she stood and threw the rag into a slop bucket.

"Brought you a little help," Galial said, pushing Laren forward.

The woman, Odes, ignored the Ishtel. "Takes forever to get anything down this baby. More food on her face than in." She was grinning, her words spoken with affection toward the baby.

Laren stood cautiously in the background, but she could see the top of the child's head. Surely this was the royal child captured from the enemy. She feared being here, especially after her experience with the red-haired royal. This was no place for an Ishtel. Yet she wanted to see the child's face.

"Take the buckets out," Odes said to Laren. She instructed her on exactly how she wanted the cloths washed in the river.

Laren stepped to the big wooden buckets by the bed, then bent to grasp the thick handles. Only then did she let her eyes fix on the child.

She was big, nearly two years old, but lying quiet. Her wide-open eyes were turned toward Laren. Yet when she looked into those little eyes, she sensed no contact. What she did see was a soft glow, a peaceful aura cast by the candles into the shadows.

Laren couldn't move. She felt as if warmth were touching her skin, penetrating her, making her take long, deep breaths.

The baby's nurse said, "Look. She's radiant."

"Yes," Galial agreed. "The babe's face is like the warm moon in a cold night."

"No, no," Odes said quickly. "The baby is always like that. I mean the Ishtel!"

Galial's head turned. "Laren?" She looked at Laren's face floating over the child. Unaware they were talking about her, the Ishtel was arched over the baby's face, transfixed. Both women watched her for a time, reluctant for their own sakes to break the spell.

Galial said to her friend, "Strange how some are so drawn to the child, and others repelled." Finally she touched Laren's arm. The young woman's head turned, as if slowly awakening. Then her hands jerked tight on the handles of the heavy buckets and she stood up with them, as if she were still only partly conscious of anything but the silent child.

The Babe in Arms

As Laren lowered the heavy buckets, they slipped slightly in her hands, nearly tipping her into the grass. She righted herself and pushed them over one at a time, dirty water and cloths rushing into the thick green bank of the river.

Bless this bucket, Laren thought. Bless this stinky wood!

It was the need for the buckets to be emptied that had brought her to the child. She was so full of gratitude she even whispered thanks for the soiled cloths and for Galial and for the child herself.

The dirty water spilling from the buckets was like her fears seeping into the soft grass under the warm sun. She picked up the soggy squares of cloth and began washing them in the river, whipping them back and forth, churning the water with them. She was full of energy, as if seeing the child had powerfully affected all the rubble within her. Gone was the dead coarseness within. Some new music beat in her—music like the motions of the river she stood in and like the grandeur of the mountains in front of her.

She gave the cloths a final rinse, snapping them in the air so that droplets flew up and then dimpled the river. After spreading them on the rocks to dry, she took off her outer rags and, with the same vigor, washed her thin discards from the refuse heaps.

In the past, always hungering to feel good about something, Laren had savored the few times she had been allowed to wash some of the royal clothing. She would think of the heroic tales and how her mother had spoken with awe about doing small favors for the great ones—how those infrequent chances gave meaning to their little lives. She would finger a dress and dream of how it had once been worn by a royal child and might soon be worn again. But the experience with the red-haired girl had soured all those feelings.

Now none of that mattered. As she scrubbed her own rags, they seemed at one with those thick, colorful clothes, and she seemed at one with the sounds of the water birds, with the gravelly bottom squishing up between her toes, even with the three slave women washing clothes downstream. She watched them talking, swishing laundry through the water, and heard their peal of laughter roll over the river's surface. She felt not fear but love for them. Love? Were her feelings love?

She felt one of the still-damp cloths and wished the sun to hurry its drying so she could carry them back to the baby.

Weighted down with a full bucket of clean water in each hand, the young Ishtel woman followed Galial, who graciously had offered to carry Laren's washed cloths. Her big bulk with the little white stack under her arm plowed past the first guards, then into the long descending corridor.

"Don't spill a drop," Galial warned as Laren struggled to keep up. "If a guard slips, he'll come after you."

Laren strained to hold the buckets steady as she walked on the uneven surface. "The child is so peaceful—"

"Some say it's the shining one's," Galial said, slowing a little. Then she told Laren the child had caused her to seek Laren out. "One day I stood looking at her and realized all my rage against you was foolish. I knew you would never again come to me, so I went out to find you."

Laren did not need to express her gratitude; both knew Galial's extraordinary lowering of herself was the most precious thing the Ishtel had ever been given.

As they neared the lower vault, they heard the baby crying. Moving past the six guards and into the chamber, Laren carefully placed the buckets by the little bed and then looked at the baby. Despite her crying, Laren felt the same peace reaching out to her. What was there about this child who lay so strangely without seeing?

"Why is she crying?"

Odes shrugged. "Babies cry. She's fed and clean."

Laren stepped a little closer and the woman said, "Her name is Meleden."

The Ishtel spoke her name, but Galial said, "She can't hear you. She can't see you, either. All she can do is move a little and cry."

Laren's hand was outstretched above the child, longing to touch her. Odes then said words unthinkable: "Reach down and pick her up."

She didn't respond, for she was drawing into herself this strange love emanating from the crying baby. The woman said it again, and Laren's brow furrowed, for she knew the woman was taking an awful risk to invite an Ishtel to touch a royal child, even an enemy royal child. Soldiers stood just outside the door. Yet now the invitation blazed in her mind, and she felt herself stooping and putting her arms under the little body that was sweaty from crying.

Lifting her took all her strength, for Meleden was surprisingly heavy. Laren stood rocking on the balls of her feet, soothing her with soft sounds, and within moments Meleden took several deep breaths and then settled into her arms and began breathing in a steady rhythm.

Holding her made tears well up in Laren's eyes; they spilled out and made moist lines down her white cheeks. She had never before held a baby. And this child, so heavy and so totally dependent and lacking everything, seemed to bring to her everything that mattered.

She looked at Galial and their eyes locked. That which had sent Galial to find her, that which had made Odes take the risk of allowing her to hold Meleden, that mysterious peace and love in this room had forged a strange bond among them all.

Laren's face, as she emerged from the dark corridors, contrasted dramatically with the rags on her body. With new eyes she looked toward the temple at the interlocking walkways, appreciating their symmetry; they looked to her like leaves beneath a flower. She studied the movements of soldiers, priests and slaves passing by the great mural that dominated the center of Belez.

It was that radiant face on the body of a ragged Ishtel that caused her trouble. She was looking clear-eyed at the city, not keeping her eyes on the ground and avoiding her betters. Suddenly a group of Mazcaen soldiers stood before her, and she was looking full into the face of one.

His look of amazement at her impertinence awakened her. But before she could turn away, he quickly stepped forward and cuffed her smartly on the side of the head, sending her sprawling to the pavement.

Reflexively, she curled into an obsequious little ball on the flat stones, ready to be kicked or yanked upright to face a vindictive mouth. But instead she heard the men walk on, for they were in a hearty mood. She listened carefully, hearing something about the coming raids on Aris. She lay still, knowing she must not rise too early and bring them back on her, nor lie so long someone else would descend upon her for cluttering up the walkway.

The fading voices spoke of booty and captives, of sacrifices in the temple to insure victory. "Only a maimed baby," she heard, and then, "Yes, but a royal one."

Maimed baby? Royal? Suddenly, for the first time since she had gazed on the child that morning, fear crept through her. For the first time in her life, it was not fear for herself. The imprint of the child's weight seemed to be still pressing on her arms. Had those voices referred to Meleden? What temple sacrifices?

She looked around at the hubbub everywhere in the city. Far more soldiers than usual, moving with brisk purpose. Always, before the legions of soldiers marched out to sack Askirit cities, she could hear temple ceremonies long into the night. She feared them. She longed to hold the strange baby once again. She felt her lightness and joy turning into dread.

Chapter 3.

──── Traders ────

Bren parted some branches, then craned his neck at the Mazcaen peak high above. Its unique shape rose above the other mountains, like a high ocean wave blown sideways. Mazcaens said the swirling stone was Mazc's pennant rippling in the wind, but the Askirit derisively called it the Broken Finger. Bren could easily think of it as a fat, gouged thumb pointing off to the side.

Below him, two traders were climbing up the trail, tall colorful baskets strapped to their backs and poking above their heads. When they came near, he stepped out and asked if he could join them. They eyed his plain brown sack of shelled corn and asked if he intended to sell that to the picky women of Belez.

"Maybe a little," he said apologetically. His clothes were like theirs but old and worn, for he wanted to be inconspicuous. "I worked a long time for this corn."

The big squarish man with a bold mustache and a richly designed basket on his back frowned. "You'll end up eating it yourself."

But they let him walk with them, and he took up the rear, quietly listening to them talk. The fancy baskets of produce bouncing on their backs were woven with bright birds and leaves and fruit. In the lower right corner of each was the symbol of the broken pole and the waving pennant, the same symbol sewn onto Bren's humble little sack.

At the city's outskirts, they made camp. Zikur, the man built like blocks of stone, laid the fire while his thin, quiet companion named Treg broke out the food and utensils. It wasn't until they had finished eating that the bigger man suddenly directed the conversation to Bren, asking a series of questions. Bren answered them easily, for he had just spent a month with a peasant family, working in their fields and earning the corn and listening intently. But then Zikur cocked his head, looking at Bren's face at various angles, and said, "You sure look Askirit to me."

Bren smiled, returning his steady gaze. "I have some Askirit blood. Some Mazcaen too. I like that. They say mongrel pups survive."

The man named Treg, who looked as if he had ancestors from many tribes, smiled back. "Mixed blood gives a man many strengths."

Zikur pulled a melon out of his basket. "Better not admit in the city that you have Askirit blood." He slashed the melon in two, then into quarters and eighths. "They call all Askirit mongrels, and they don't mean it kindly."

The Askirit had intermarried widely, so it was true their dark copper skin came in many shades and their features greatly varied; in contrast to the Mazcaens.

Bren accepted two slices and said, like a boy who knew nothing at all, "I hear the Mazcaens are planning raids. Does that mean they're out looking for sacrifices?"

The big man gave him another long, studied look. "They have plenty of sacrifices. Captives. Slaves. And peasants like you who do something really stupid."

Treg glared at Bren. "Like insult the wrong person." He warned that at the market in Belez even a slave might be buying for a royal family. "You can haggle. But you always back down if you see that hard edge coming into their faces."

Zikur swore. "And if one of the royal women is there, just beg for an honest price and take what she gives."

Bren tried to get them back to the subject of sacrifices and asked about captives. "With all the Askirit royalty killed in the quake, the raids must—"

"Not all the Askirit royalty died," Treg interrupted. "You couldn't walk these roads and not hear something about the baby and the curse."

Bren chewed slowly, as if not overly interested. "The gods were upset, I heard. The baby signaled the queen's fate."

"Yup." Zikur was still appraising him, his eyes on Bren even when he took a long drink of water.

Bren decided to take a risk anyway by saying, "Yet some say the baby wasn't a curse at all. That celestial ones hover all around her."

Zikur laughed, wrinkling his face. "Should be interesting when they sacrifice her!"

Bren's head jerked toward him. Zikur leaned back expansively. "It's no secret. A hundred captives to die with the child. Sacrifices to prepare for the attacks on Aris and Kelerai."

Bren knew Zikur had watched his eyes tighten at the news. "Sorry about your Askirit blood," Zikur said with the hint of a leer.

Busying himself by pulling hot corn off the fire, then gingerly stuffing a little into his mouth, Bren said with a careful smile, "My Mazcaen blood loves it."

— In the City —

Bren wanted his sack of corn back. A woman had spied it beside him as his companions were selling their produce in the market. She had demanded it, stuffing the money into his hand, then had yanked the sack up on her shoulder and walked away.

Zikur and Treg had congratulated him on a fair price, but he feared not having the sack to identify him as a trader. Now, as they walked in the early morning toward the city's center, his companions' empty baskets rode high above their heads and he felt vulnerable to the glances of passing soldiers and priests.

They walked a lower path close by the river, where slave women were washing; Bren noticed a small figure in rags, bent over two very fancy white buckets. Rectangular cloths were spread around her drying on the rocks. "How odd," he said, "that shabby girl rinsing out those buckets with the royal insignias. Where would she get those?"

"Looks like the Ishtel's washing diapers," Zikur said, his nose curled in disgust. "Maybe they have her tending that Askirit baby."

Bren was nearly past her and at Zikur's words jerked his head back to look at her again. She had risen slightly, tipping water from one of the buckets, and the sun glinted from her golden hair. He desperately wanted to go to her, but his companions kept walking and he could not think of a reason to break away; he felt conspicuous without them and kept walking, but stole glances back at the small figure until she was out of sight.

They turned a corner into a vast panorama of walkways leading like an artful spider web toward the murals and temple. "Mazcaen kings all look alike," Zikur said, nodding his head toward the great mosaic figures marching toward the city's center. He and Treg were both nervous, for they had wanted to conclude their business and get out. They had told him that Belez was not a place to stroll around and gawk; they would walk with him just once past the mural and temple.

Bren tried stalling them anyway, trying to stay on the walk closest to the river so he could see the girl again. He told himself he was an idiot for not finding a way to get to her, that if Zikur were right, he had to talk to this girl. Yet he couldn't just go off alone.

The traders loved explaining the city's symbols, and Bren listened as if he had never heard any of it. How the Mazcaen survivors beneath the surface had never forgotten their kings. On them the small Mazcaen culture had persisted in the darkness below, and when a small band had finally emerged, they had searched everywhere for their sacred peak. Finding this one, they declared it the holy mountain and proceeded to create the larger-than-life murals.

Bren's eyes were darting everywhere, appraising the people on the walkways, studying the temple and the complex of buildings. He noticed those of rank entered under massive arches in front, but the slaves followed narrowing walkways leading, surely, to lower entrances.

They had left the lower walk but he kept looking backward, stalling them with questions, until finally he noticed the small figure far behind. She was walking resolutely—almost jauntily, with the dry buckets in her hands—completely unlike an Ishtel.

She crossed over to another walkway, moving rapidly. He felt he had to take a risk and said, "She sure doesn't walk like an Ishtel. Look at her!"

He had interrupted one of Zikur's explanations, which annoyed him. "I don't look around at Ishtels."

Bren watched her, trying to figure out how to intersect her path without making a spectacle of himself. Zikur made an earthy remark about what Ishtels were good for. The ragged young woman was moving out of his sight. Bren bolted away, determined to reach her.

He walked swiftly, barely glancing at her, trying to look as if he were looking up at the kings towering gloriously above. His heart raced, knowing anyone might notice his quickened pace. Her bobbing form was starting to disappear down one of the narrowing paths and he sped up even more. Reaching a set of stairs, he almost ran down them; the walkways were well behind him when he finally caught sight of her again. She heard his footsteps and increased her pace.

"Wait!" he commanded.

She stopped in mid-stride as suddenly as if a spear had spitted her against the wall. She did not turn her head as he briskly came up behind her. She stood with eyes to the ground, faded rags clinging to her body, long hair partially hiding her face.

All his life Bren had heard about Ishtels, but he had never seen one before—so light-skinned, with golden hair contrasting with his dark curls. Now that he had caught up to her and she was standing stiff as a statue, he didn't know what to say. Reaching out, he parted her hair with his hand and gently raised her face. "I only want to talk to you."

She would not look at him; her eyes stayed fixed low on the wall ahead, buckets hanging from her hands. He stared down at her delicate, strange features with more fascination than he had felt toward the city's murals and causeways. She was a fantasy creature come alive; it was as if one of those alluring yet innocent girls of woods and water had stepped out of a children's tale and was frozen in front of him.

He reached down to still the slight trembling of her chin, but she cringed at his touch.

"I won't hurt you," he said as gently as he could. Then, as if a voice whispered to him, he sensed he should take the risk, "I only want to know about the Askirit baby."

Her eyes flashed up, for a split instant drilled into his, then dropped again—but not before he had seen her alarm and agony.

Footsteps sounded above them. She urgently waved him off and quickly began moving away. "I want to save the child," he called softly after her.

He pulled out his small rabbit-skin map of the city, studied it and acted lost, waiting for the footsteps to reach him, hoping this was not someone who had noticed his rapid movements. As the steps come closer, he turned and looked with a stupid expression at the Mazcaen soldier marching toward him.

"It was an Ishtel!" he declared, as if explaining a rare phenomenon. He knew if the soldier had seen him crossing the walkways he'd have to explain that first. Bren lowered his jaw like a simpleton. "She didn't speak to me. Just like the great kings out there! No one speaks here." He held up his map and waved it in front of the man in mystification.

The big soldier studied him with his jaw firmly set.

"Are all Ishtels ladies?" Bren asked, eyes big, mouth open wide and head tilted with utmost sincerity.

He asked several more inane questions until the soldier said between tight lips, "You have Askirit blood."

Bren answered immediately, his face breaking into a huge smile. "Yes. That's right! That's what mother always says. 'A lot of Mazcaen, a little Askirit, and far too much barbarian!'" He kept smiling broadly, as if very proud of his recitation.

The soldier asked more questions, and Bren said he'd come to sell his sack of corn for his family and now was allowed to see the city. He acted as if he were delighted the soldier was paying attention to him. "See, here's the money!" Bren reached into his pocket and pulled out the carved shells he'd received. "A big woman in long white clothes just bought it all," he said, his mouth stretched wide in a cherubic, satisfied circle.

The Strange Visitor

Laren wanted to bolt from the strange peasant and the approaching footsteps, but she forced herself to walk at a steady pace. She passed through familiar tunnels but then paused at the doorway where she hoped to meet Galial, her heart still pumping rapidly. She didn't want Galial to realize she was distraught.

The soldiers might come down here for her. Those footsteps sounded like a soldier's. Should she go out through another entrance? But if they wanted her, that might look even worse, and they could easily track her down. Better to go in to Galial.

What had the man wanted? Had she been implicated?

His words kept coming back. "I want to save the child." Who would want to save the child? How could she possibly be saved?

She breathed deeply several times, then stepped into the room. Holding her hands tightly together to steady them, she walked to Galial and asked in her usual obsequious manner if she should now go to help with the child. Galial motioned her to follow.

They were standing by Meleden's little bed before Laren chanced a comment. "People talk about many captives being sacrificed."

Galial grunted assent, lifting the child into her arms and speaking to her. The baby swallowed and shifted her head a little, but as her eyes moved, they didn't focus on anything.

Laren forced out her next words like a mouthful of bad meat. "Some say the child will be sacrificed with them."

Galial gave her a sharp, indignant look, but then looked back at the baby. She carried her to a chair in which she sat down heavily, adjusting Meleden in her arms. "Clean up the bed," she instructed the Ishtel.

Laren bent over and pulled the blankets off, then turned with them in her arms, looking at Galial. She saw in her face that it was true.

Galial said, "Many a child's bones lie under the altar. Her fate is not in our hands."

Yet the child's body was in Galial's arms. Both of them had sensed extraordinary peace within her. How could they, who cared for her, have nothing at all to do with her fate?

Laren finished the work and stood beside the soiled blankets and the buckets, ready to take them out. Galial stood, walked to her, and handed her the child. "Sit down for a time with her."

Laren held the heavy baby tightly against her chest, the large head in the cradle of her shoulder. "What will happen to you?" she asked the baby who could not see or hear.

Laren had fiercely attacked the job of washing the blankets as if she were strangling a resisting enemy. She had exhausted herself lunging up and down in the river with the heavy, sodden blankets, shaking them furiously, then with her palms beating the water out of them on the rocks.

Now she stared at them drying under the hot noon sun, little cloths spread around them. Her muscles were pleasantly tired but her feelings and thoughts chaotic. She did not hear anyone approaching on the grass until the man's voice softly said, "I won't hurt you. I'm here to help."

The sound was like scalding water. Her chin dropped and her fingers dug into the dirt beneath the grass. This man could get her beaten to death on the spot. She wanted to hiss, "Get out!" But an Ishtel never said that to anyone but another Ishtel.

"Do you care about the child?" She felt his hand grasp her shoulder, turning her slightly toward him. "You may be the only person who can save her."

She raised her head a little but wouldn't steal even a glance upward. "Save her from what?"

"You know. They will streak her with paints, and they will lead her into the chamber of the kings, and to the altar of lions' teeth above the bones of other sacrifices. All the city is abuzz."

She said nothing. He plied her with questions, about how often she saw the child and what she did in there and who else cared about the child.

"I never said I cared about the child. Your talking with me will put us under the interrogators."

With both hands he slowly lifted her face so that she had to look at him. His dark hands on her flesh were alien, frightening. He was young, intense, full lips pressed together, neither slave nor Mazcaen but a mixture like other traders. "I know the dangers," he assured her. His eyes were like dark-bronze suns burning into hers. "But I have been touched by the child. I have held Meleden in my arms."

She turned from him and fingered the blankets. They were still a bit damp, but she picked one up anyway, standing with it and holding it high to make the first fold.

"Let me help."

She looked at the man as if she had been slapped. A trader help an Ishtel? That would alert everyone. She was glad to see his eyes warily scanning the balconies above.

"Meleden is the Maker's gift to us," he said urgently. "We must get her away from here."

So he was an Askirit spy. He had to be. He was a man everyone in Belez would hate.

The realization appalled her even as it became suddenly clear that Meleden might actually be saved. The thought filled her with a terrible mixture of hope and fear.

——— Refuse Heaps ———

Bren tried to control his shaking hands. The tension of being so close to getting caught for so long was affecting his nerves, muscles, stomach. He had left the Ishtel girl when he'd seen soldiers looking down at them and now he berated himself for not staying longer, pressing her about what the child meant to her and to think about how they might rescue her. Yet she had seemed frightened, unresponsive.

He kept scanning the city for anyone staring at him, and if he thought someone might be, he headed elsewhere. He didn't want to act like a simpleton again; it had barely worked with the soldier. He had purchased in the market a big pack decorated with colorful birds and, of course, the pennant symbol. He had stuffed it full of food and little tools, but he still felt conspicuous.

Now he stood between the refuse heaps and the barren rocks where he was told the Ishtels congregated. He was fascinated by them, for among the Askirit the plight of the Ishtels was one more way they depicted the Mazcaen culture as abhorrent.

He saw the girl coming over a ridge, then striding down toward the heaps by the river. It was true, she did not move diffidently like other Ishtels. The quick clicking of stones in her hands was lively, spirited. She hopped over a pile of rocks instead of slowly walking around them.

His pulse raced as he watched her. Were his feelings simply from being on the stark edge of getting caught and knowing this young woman was the key to everything? No, it was more. Her rags stirred as the wind caught their edges, her hair lifted above her forehead. She was incongruously lovely.

He quietly walked close to her. She was squatting, her teeth sunk into a fish bone. Hearing him, she jerked herself erect, her lips pursed tightly in angry surprise.

But it was his voice, not hers, that expressed outrage. "Don't they even feed you for all your work?"

She bent down and picked up the backbone and head of a fish that had been lying in the sun. "Only sometimes." She bit down savagely. "A little corn now and then."

"Can't you fish in the river instead of—"

"Ishtels can't fish! Or hunt. Or plant. They can just pick."

He pulled the pack off his back and found some baked grains shaped into tiny loaves. He offered her one, and she hesitated for only a moment before taking it and gulping it down. He gave her several more and she ate them all.

Bren was fascinated by the girl's eyes, darting nervously like little bluebirds from one spot to another. He noticed a splash of tiny freckles that broke over the base of her finely chiseled little nose. He had never seen freckles before, and he had never seen such blue eyes before. When they finally paused for a moment in a steady look into his, he saw in them passages to mysteries he longed to understand.

"Have you thought more about saving the child?" he asked.

"I never said I would think about it." Her eyes were down again; she walked to the river and began washing her hands.

"Saving the child would bring you a whole new life. You're a beautiful young woman. You need food and clothes."

She angrily shook the water from her hands. "Why do you mock me?"

"I am not mocking!"

She sneered. "Then you're repulsive. Lots of men have mocked me for being ugly, but to say I'm beautiful just so you can get me to help you—that's despicable." She tilted her fish-oily face up toward him and hissed. "I am not beautiful, and I will not help you."

She sank back down, like a water bag suddenly emptied, and he sat beside her. She turned away to scrub her face.

The river sparkled under the early afternoon sun and he stared at it. "You're the only hope the baby has."

She stretched out on her back, eyes squinted shut against the drying rays.

"My name is Bren," he offered.

She toyed with some pebbles in her hand, but she didn't click them or tap them together.

"Among those who love the child are Askirit women ready to face any danger. They are called Enre. They are spiritual, like you. And like them, you understand about the child."

She said nothing.

"Strange wonders are beginning. Strange blessings touch those who embrace the child."

She finally sat up and looked at him; he felt as if she were evaluating every nuance of his face. "Go back to Aris," she said. "You can't do anything. The guards said the priests will come tomorrow to get her."

A Little Violence

Next morning, Laren went as usual straight to Galial, but instead of waiting to see if she would accompany her to the child, Laren handed her a note. She stood quietly as Galial read it, then nodded when told she could leave.

Laren often went alone to the child's room; the guards had gotten used to her daily routine and never challenged her. After all, she was only an Ishtel.

She wondered if they had taken the child yet. As she entered the room, Laren wasn't sure what she wanted to see. If the baby's bed were empty, she could leave and forget all these horrifying plans in her head. Yet that would mean little Meleden would be soon painted for destruction.

The child was in the bed, lying on her back, eyes wide open. A little thrill ran down Laren's back. But, she thought, the worst part of what I'm to do is right now.

She nodded to Odes and walked over to the slop buckets. "Just a little violence," Bren had said to her. "It will protect her, for she'll be found unconscious and won't be blamed. Can you think of any other way?" He had told her how to do it without killing her.

Killing her? Was she actually thinking these thoughts? Was her body actually going to obey the images in her mind?

She bent over and dragged out the full buckets. As she walked past the bed to get the empty ones, she removed the heavy wooden block under her clothes. Then, in the motion she had practiced again and again in the woods, she abruptly turned, lifted her body above the nurse, struck her hard, then grabbed her before she could fall.

Odes had cried out a little as she was struck, but Laren had said loudly as she caught her, "Hush, baby! Hush baby! We have to move your bed a little." She eased Odes into the chair, turning it so the woman was facing the bed, her back to the doorway. Laren arranged her hair and pulled her into a sitting position.

A little violence? How could she strike her friend? How could an Ishtel be involved in such things? Yet how could she let this baby be murdered?

Bren had said of heroic stories, "Did you think the great ones were sure of success? No, what they attempted seemed impossible! Often treasonous, always nasty, most likely fatal."

She had no desire to be a heroine; she wanted only to protect the life she felt from the baby, wanted only to keep her from the violence these great ones had in store for her. She pulled the small blanket from the bed and stuffed it like an eggshell into an empty bucket. Then she lifted the infant and carefully sat her in the bucket. She took the larger blanket and placed it on top of her, tossed the other blanket on a full bucket, and lifted them both.

Satisfied that she looked the same as she always did when she emerged from the room, she approached the doorway, giving a brief glance back at Odes. A patch of blood showed where she had been hit. Bren had assured her she would survive; Laren fervently hoped so.

The six guards blocked the way like a thick door of flesh. She coughed as usual to be let past, for she never spoke to them. They turned, talking among themselves, and she walked between them, trying to even out the weight between the water and the heavier bucket carrying the baby.

What if Meleden cried, even whimpered? She and Bren had talked about maybe gagging her, but both had thought it would only upset her and surely make her more noisy. No, it would be a miracle if she were silent all the way, and that was what Bren had been praying with her for as they had talked long into the night.

Meleden was silent in the bucket and Laren was a full three paces past the guards when the uneven balance caused her to slop some water onto the floor.

"Clean that up!"

The words could have been icy blades thrusting through her back. They immobilized her. Gently she eased the buckets down. She couldn't leave them here and go back for some cloths to clean up the spill. Yet she couldn't ignore an order and just keep walking.

She stooped with her fingers on the buckets, her mind jumbled with useless thoughts. She was trapped, her face hot, her hands sweating. She prayed to the Maker that Bren had invoked, praying the baby would not so much as sigh. She thought of the baby. She thought of the love she felt from the child, and she fixed her mind on that and the life the baby seemed always surrounded by. And it came into her mind to say, in utmost humility with her back still to the guards, "Please, first may I take the buckets outside? You don't want them near you—today, they stink something awful!"

One guard laughed but another roared, "Then move them down the hall a little, but clean up that mess!"

She lifted her heavy burdens, commanding her arms to stop trembling and shaking the buckets. She walked ahead as far as she thought they would let her, eased the buckets down again with extreme care, then turned and rapidly passed the guards, saying, "Have to get dry cloths."

Going back into the room was like forcing herself back into a flaming building. Odes was sprawled on the chair like a drunk, a narrow rivulet of blood running down the side of her face and onto the chair. She walked past her, grabbed a big pile of dry cloths and spun around with them piled from her navel to her chin.

As she came out the door, she realized she had taken too many. What would she do with all these after she had cleaned up the spill? But she kept moving.

She got on her knees and hurriedly swabbed up the spill. The guards made lewd suggestions about how she should do the job, but their words meant nothing to her. All her concerns were on the baby. Any instant she expected a cry and her prayers were bursts of agony.

The floor was dry. She picked up the big pile of cloths, half of them not even wet, and started toward the bucket.

"Where are you taking all those? You didn't use half of them!"

She stopped dead at his voice, as she knew she must. Finally she said, "I'll wash them all fresh."

The man snorted but did not order her back, so she tentatively started forward again. She wondered if she were making a huge mistake; how could she get all these balanced on top of the buckets? Yet she couldn't, just couldn't, go back into that room.

She balanced half the diapers on each bucket and wedged them in with the handles, barely having room to get her fingers between. Then she pulled up, praying her trembling arms would not betray her again. Slowly she moved down the corridor, calling for every reserve of energy to keep steady, and when she turned the corner at the stairs, she went part way up and put the buckets down. She tossed all the extras to the floor, dumped half the water from the full one, then fiercely grabbed the handles and charged up the stairs, wanting open air like a diver deep under water.

Bren watched her from the woods as she labored down the hill with the buckets. Any observer could have seen what made him so anxious: her shaking body made it look as if she would surely drop the buckets. Bren was grateful no one in Belez paid any attention to Ishtels. He wanted to run up the hill and help her, but he planted his feet firmly in place, his whole body straining with her every movement.

Step by laborious step he watched her head down toward the meeting of grass, forest and river. Was the sun still moving? Had the world stopped? Everything seemed maddeningly slowed as he waited for angry shouts to accost her on the hill.

As soon as she was one step into the woods, he reached for the buckets and quickly carried them several paces further in. She stumbled after him as he carefully reached under the blankets and lifted the baby free. She was heavy in his hands but wonderfully light to his spirit, her eyes wide open and her mouth making little grunts.

"Did she make any noise?" He motioned for her to sit down, then placed her in her arms.

"None. Not once."

Bren grabbed the buckets, drained the one, quickly filled both with rocks he had piled up nearby, then dropped them into the river. He helped Laren up, reached for Meleden, and said, "You lead."

She startled him by bolting off down the forest trail in a blur of rags and legs. He had barely gotten his arm around the baby and stumbled after her, trying to juggle Meleden on his hip and worrying he'd lose sight of the trail at his feet. Yet the exhilaration of having the child in his arms and running free through the woods made him understand why Laren must have been so instantly relieved and refreshed. He saw her flying feet far ahead disappearing over a rise. He renewed his speed but worried about stumbling, gained the rise, but then lost the trail.

He stood there a moment panting and was relieved to see Laren in the distance running back, then beckoning. He raced forward again and was completely out of breath by the time he caught up to her standing at the forest's edge.

"There's the market," she said, stroking the baby on his heaving chest. "Galial's up there. The big woman in red on this side."

He placed the child in Laren's arms, waited another instant to get his breath, then started up the hill toward the woman. He asked himself with every step if he was making a major blunder, for he was jeopardizing the rescue just when they were likely to get away. But he kept walking up the hill and caught Galial's eye when she turned in his direction.

Laren watched them talking, worried that instead of rescuing Galial she might be making them all die more swiftly.

The night before, when Bren had said Galial would surely be accused of treason and killed, she had pressed him hard. They had to send Galial on a wild goose chase anyway, so why not send her here, then take her with them? Bren had resisted the idea. As Laren stood with the baby in her arms watching them talk, she remembered his every objection. The alarm might be sounded while he was trying to get her to come down. Galial could get suspicious and call out.

What would Laren do if soldiers nabbed him up there? Here she was with the baby, not knowing anything about the trails beyond Belez. She'd be instantly caught.

Yet as she looked down on the child, she felt a strange assurance that she was doing what she was called to do, that the deep breaths she kept taking were being strangely blessed.

Money had been with the note she had handed Galial, along with the promise of meeting someone very important. Was Galial suspicious now? Why were they taking so long up there?

At last they began moving down the hill, and she could see Bren was trying to hurry the big woman. When they finally got close to Laren, Bren stopped. "Actually, I'm not a trader," he said. "I'm an Askirit spy."

She saw Galial roll her eyes in exasperation. She had obviously been doubtful about Bren, and now this bizarre statement. She leaned back and drew breath to give a heated reply when Laren coughed, the way she would cough so the guards would let her by. Galial recognized the sound behind the trees and her eyes flashed in that direction. She saw Laren and the baby in her arms, and her face collapsed in astonishment.

"Call out, and we're all dead together! Move into the woods," Bren commanded.

Galial moved toward Laren, stricken dumb, a volcano of white-faced fury and terror.

"We've rescued the child," Laren said. "We knew you'd be blamed, so we came for you." She reached out for Galial's hand and pressed it against the back of the child's head.

"Your only choice is to come with us," Bren said, pushing the women deeper into the forest. "You're more fortunate than you think, Galial. You'll earn freedom with us and the child—if we can get out of Belez."

Chapter 4.

—— The Peak ——

The fugitives moved swiftly beyond the city's walls, Bren carrying the baby under one arm like a military sack. He charged onto a rocky trail leading upward and the two women scrambled after him.

Laren was amazed that her terror kept her climbing faster and longer than she thought possible. But suddenly the trail stopped at a sheer wall. Galial slumped onto a pile of rocks, breathing heavily. Laren, leaning her sweaty back against a boulder, tenderly explored a new bruise on her calf.

"Where are we going?" Galial demanded.

"To the peak." Bren had already shifted Meleden to his other arm and was starting up a jagged crevice.

Galial was horrified. "We can't go all the way up there! No one can go up there."

"That's why we will," Bren said, already moving out of sight.

Laren stared and finally climbed after him, but she felt a dark dread. The peak was nothing to fool with. Did Bren realize what could happen up here? Was he such a stranger that he didn't know the tales? It couldn't be for nothing that no one in all Belez would think of desecrating the peak.

Yet here she was climbing it, for she couldn't let Bren and the baby disappear.

She heard Galial's angry grunts far behind and slowed just a little, keeping Bren in view. She felt angry at Bren for racing them into strange terrors, but she also felt relief that their pursuers would never search for them up here.

At the top of the mountain, weathered formations poked up all across the rambling plateau, creating weird shapes and deep gullies. Bren was wriggling through one, somehow going ever higher and higher. Finally he stood nearly at the top, just beneath the wind-blasted rock that rose straight up, then tipped crazily to the side.

Laren stared in wonder. So this was the Pennant itself!

Bren was poking his head up over the formation's peak when she climbed up behind him. He handed her the baby. "She's been crying some, but I think she's fine." He scooted himself up a half-step higher. "There are still rocks behind us, so even if the Mazcaens look up, they won't see us against the sky."

Laren sat exhausted, the baby cradled in her arms. As she began to cool off, she drew Meleden closer, hugging her for warmth against the darkening chill. "Won't we freeze up here? We can't make a fire."

"Yes, we can. There's a very deep cleft, deep enough so they can't see the flames, and at night they won't see smoke."

"You've been here before?"

"Many times." He stepped down to her. "Troops are still leaving the city. Probably searching every trail and hamlet for us."

Galial finally reached them. She slumped down, breathing in deep, quick gasps, wiping her face with her sleeve. Laren had never seen her so distraught, not since the royal child had accosted her. She was glaring at Bren, like a bear run to exhaustion by hunters but still belligerent.

Bren walked to her, glaring back. "Would you rather be on the torturer's rack? We took a huge risk for you."

She took a long, shuddering breath. "I can't be on this mountain."

"You're on it!"

Her fists were mercilessly squeezing her own thumbs. "It's almost night. We'll never see the dawn. How does it help the child to bring her here to die?"

Bren shrugged. "I've spent many a night on this peak." He turned his back and climbed up to look at the city in the evening shadows.

Laren knew what Galial was feeling. Every day of both their lives, the peak had looked down on them, full of menace yet promise, full of power and terrible mystery.

When Bren came back down Galial said, "Maybe for you, an Askirit spy, it doesn't matter. But for me, this mountain cannot be violated!"

He locked his eyes on hers. "Would you let them sacrifice the child? Meleden is so full of life it spills out of her. Would you hand her over?"

Galial averted her eyes. "Sacrifices must be. They are seed; they avert disasters." But she said this with no conviction.

He dropped down to sit on his haunches in front of her. "We've all been touched by the child." He took the baby from Laren, gently pressing her against his chest for a moment. Then he placed her into Galial's arms. "She's a gift. She's like a tree planted in a river, parting the souls of all who touch her." He stroked the child's cheek on Galial's shoulder. "I know you're terrified up here. But once I saw the world from much higher up, on the fringes of death with the celestials. I've lost all such terror."

Laren was studying Bren's face, trying to make sense of what he was saying. He began talking about evil and battles and wars. She didn't follow his meanings, but she liked what he had said about Meleden, and the way he had held the child.

——— The Trail ———

Bren loved looking down from the peak at the people and animals moving far below in the city and on distant trails. It reminded him of the moments he had looked down from even higher up as the celestials filled his mind with wonders. Whenever the old timidity started seeping back in, he thought again about those moments; they now flavored everything he experienced. He sensed that in the end, no matter what happened, all would be well. Even as he looked down on enemies longing to torture him, he felt remarkably little fear. Instead, he felt that same humor bubbling up that the celestials had seemed so full of, and he climbed down from his perch with a broad smile on his face.

"Smile now," Galial said. "The trails may be grim."

"Maybe so." They had spent many tense days on the peak watching the search below. But the last two days, the traffic of traders and soldiers looked more normal, and he saw no one using the obscure trail he intended to take. "Let's find out just how grim," he said. "We'll never be more ready than now."

They had constantly talked about how to avoid detection. He had told them, "If we're caught, no matter how many there are, we might win by surprising them." Then he had handed each a hefty blade.

Galial had been astounded that he would give a blade to an Ishtel. Even worse, he began to train her in its use—a capital crime in Belez. But after a time, the big slave woman had swallowed one more outrage and had concentrated with her companions on how to survive their improbable flight.

Even so, as they prepared to leave, a new confrontation turned ugly. As Bren adjusted his pack and then hefted an additional basket of food, Galial handed Laren her water sack and cloak. Bren eyed her sharply. "You planning on carrying the baby?"

"Why? I'm carrying plenty."

He glanced at Laren who already wore a pack and held the big baby in her arms. "The one with the baby carries less."

Galial glared at him, and he strained to be tactful. "Let's take turns carrying Meleden and the extra gear. Laren's pretty small, so—"

Bren's tact hit Galial like a rock slide. "An Ishtel has her place!" The big woman stuck her face nose to nose against Bren's. "You think you're Laren's protector? Let me tell you, I was the first to say a kind word to her. I was the one who put the baby into her arms. I was the one to put food into her mouth."

She lowered her head like a bull, straining her eyes up at him. "The Ishtel almost got me killed! Anyone but me would never have looked at her again. But I went after her—actually went looking for her!" Galial's lips were trembling. "You think you can set everyone straight. But you're just an Askirit spy! They'll dissect you one small piece at a time."

He stepped two full paces back, starting to say they'd do the same to her, when Laren stepped between them. "When Galial sought me out among the Ishtels, I was astounded." She slung the water bottle and cloak over one shoulder and lifted the baby onto the other.

Bren glowered at Galial, then studied the slight young woman burdened like a pack animal. He grunted, the smile long gone, and started leading the way down, determined very soon to take the water bottle and cloak himself.

They moved in silence over the narrow trail that looped far into the forest, then back toward the Askirit cities. Despite their loads, they covered a long distance quickly, breaking out of the forest about noon and moving over open, rocky spaces between clumps of trees. Always they were listening for their pursuers.

Then the baby started crying. The sounds ripped through all of them. At Meleden's first whimper, they ducked into a grove.

"Feed her!" Galial commanded, although Laren already had a piece of soft cheese in her mouth. The baby spat it out and cried more loudly.

"Must be our fast pace," Bren said.

Laren recalled holding the buckets beside the guards, trembling at the thought of Meleden's making a sound. Now she felt the same way. Here they were in a forest full of soldiers hunting them, and the baby split the air with unnerving sounds. They could hide hundreds of places, but the baby's cry would lead their pursuers anywhere they hid. Laren was rocking her, cuddling her, shushing her, trying to get food or water into her, but Meleden was wrenching her head back and forth, crying the louder. Everything upset her, as if she were very uncomfortable and determined to tell the world about it.

"Let's keep moving," Bren said. "Might as well."

They hustled over the trail, sweating with exertion, knowing they were as exposed by her cries as if they were strolling on a bald mountain. Laren had never thought about how vulnerable Meleden's cries would make them. But babies cried; how could the child know?

They first saw the soldiers far below them near a string of boulders. They were looking up, as if hearing Meleden, and then they disappeared into the trail.

Bren just stood there, staring down.

Galial shifted her pack. "Let's move!"

Bren was surveying all the trails up and down, taking deep breaths, grinding his teeth. The baby's wails were sirens in their ears, unerring guides for their pursuers.

Finally Bren said to Laren, pointing to a formation jutting out like a gargoyle far above them, "Climb with Meleden up there." He pulled off Laren's pack and threw it into the bushes. "Leave everything else here." Then he tossed his own gear after Laren's and said, "Galial, we'll go down to that steep incline. Bring weapons only."

Laren saw a look of dismay cross Galial's face. It was soon replaced by grim determination.

A moment later Laren was racing up the rocky trail, babe in arms, still trying to quiet her as she climbed.

Ambush, she thought. Bren and Galial will ambush them. They'll hear Meleden crying with me way up here and never suspect two are waiting for them. But two against all those soldiers?

She climbed more slowly now, not as desperate about the crying. By the time she reached the formation, she was not breathing so heavily. She spied a deep, wooded ravine close by and followed a deer trail to its edge. Gripping a big oak on its very rim, she looked down the sheer drop of sandstone cliffs. Not far beneath, just a little way down under leaning hardwoods and pines, were shallow caves. She worked her way down, then searched among them until she found a dry one thick with soft needles and leaves.

Easing herself down on her back, she positioned Meleden on her chest, letting her sob, humming quietly to her, trying to soothe both the child and herself.

In a surprisingly short time, Meleden's breathing became more and more regular. She lay on Laren heavy and warm, one small hand squeezing and releasing her shoulder until it was still.

What was going on below? She had left her companions a long time ago, and she had heard nothing. Perhaps soldiers were even now just above her, ready to seize her. She tried to keep planning what to do if surprised by the pursuers, but as she lay with Meleden asleep on her chest, she began to feel peaceful. Her thoughts lifted with the sight of great trees all around her rising from ravine and cliff, fighting to secure a hold in the thin topsoil. The only sounds were the rapid breathing of the child and her own. Somehow they seemed joined, her heart beating slowly now, with that rapid little heart on her breast. Laren felt fully part of this child's mysterious drama.

Her hand stroking Meleden slowed and then fell to her side.

At first the images of her dream were veiled and indistinct. Her emotions were still lifted like the trees around her, lifted with the child. Always before Meleden had entered her life, she had been on the periphery; now she felt at the heart of something magnificently meaningful.

Deep, lovely woods appeared in her dream. A man sat on a bench under a birch with leaves of autumn colors. He held something in his lap.

Laren stepped closer; it was Meleden he held.

The man was bent over her, whispering in her ear, smiling. At Laren's approach, he looked up with the same smile, and only then did she see that he was horribly crippled. He looked as if he had lived through an accident that should have killed him. His body was bent and twisted; in contrast, Meleden seemed whole and perfect, lying with a little smile, her head in the crook of his arm.

She suddenly sensed enormous power from this crippled, shrunken man was radiating into her. He was rising by use of a cane, one arm supporting the little child, and beckoned her closer with a toss of his head.

"You're an Ishtel?" He wasn't asking but looked bemused, as if he knew her well. "Yes, an Ishtel!" He said it as if this were very pleasing.

Meleden moved in his arms; he smiled and shifted her toward Laren.

She took her and felt a warm energy in her arms.

The man leaned against the birch trunk. "Laren. Laren." He said her name as if savoring its sound. "Laren. The Ishtel I love."

Love? What was drawing her to him, for Meleden had been taken from her by some shining figure and now Laren was bringing the cripple something in her hands. She opened her fists and looked down. They were rocks. Small and large, polished and rough. They began floating out of her hands and into the air; men appeared, shining men, and they took the rocks in their own hands and made wonderful music. She wanted to sing with them, but she could not, for she couldn't grasp the words or even hum along.

She looked at her hands. They were full again. She opened them, and this time they held greasy bones, rotten cloth, and wormy kernels of corn.

The strange man took them from her, and as he did, she saw something new. She hadn't noticed how ragged his clothes were. He looked very much like an Ishtel. The man took a bone in his wounded, deformed hand and gnawed on it. Then he stuffed the ruined corn into his mouth. The old cloth she had held he placed on his knee where his skin showed through a wide split in his rags.

He took Meleden in one arm again; the baby had a beatific smile on her face, and the shining ones were laughing with infectious joy.

The cripple motioned her closer, but she felt unworthy and soiled, for despite his appearance, he seemed more celestial and shining than the music makers. He moved to her, Meleden in one arm, and kissed her cheek; she felt something go through her, something cleansing and empowering.

Slowly the strange, ragged man leaned back against the white birch, red and yellow and black leaves lazily falling around his feet. He pitched away his cane, beckoning Laren to him so he could hug her and Meleden together. She felt held so firmly by his wounded arm she sensed he would never let go, never, never let her fall. The cripple felt like father, brother, lover, friend.

Meleden's face resting on his chest was close beside hers; the child's smile said she understood so much more than Laren did.

Laren awakened to see Meleden's little mouth slightly open just above her, eyes shut, tiny lashes still. Laren wanted to hold on to the wonderful feelings from her dream. She shut her eyes again, but when she heard a squirrel rustling, opened them to study Meleden's face. She lay there a long time, trying to remember every part of the dream and seal it into her memory.

But her predicament invaded her thoughts. Bren and Galial had been long gone. Soldiers were surely hunting them. What now?

She could retrieve the packs, but the baby would most likely cry again before she could escape the forests. And escape to where? Even if she got to the Askirit kingdom, she couldn't just walk up to someone and say, "Here's your kidnapped baby." They'd probably spear her on the spot.

Yet looking up at the small face, so innocent and powerful— yes, powerful, like the dream—she felt part of that purity and purpose. She was in league with this child. Even if they were captured and killed, she was in league with her, and they would fulfill their purpose.

As Meleden started to awaken, Laren decided to get the packs, determined to make her way to the coast. She could do it. She was an Ishtel, a survivor.

She was already out of the shelter and nearly back at the formation that Bren had pointed out when she heard him calling her name.

That night they camped in a deep ravine far from the trails, denying themselves fire, speaking only in whispers. Laren told them nothing about the dream, letting them tell her in a rush of words how they had toppled boulders on the five pursuers, then attacked them. Galial brandished her blade and described with relish how she had dispatched a man just about to stab her. Laren barely listened, trying to keep her sense of unique purpose intact, savoring the feelings that had started in Belez when she had first held Meleden in her arms.

Deep into the night, as they lay under the stars, Bren was still telling Laren about his plans and why he had come on this mission, all the while asking her questions that she dodged. Galial was already sleeping nearby and Laren was ready to join her. She couldn't understand why Bren wanted to talk to her so much; she wanted to close her eyes and think about the dream and Meleden. But he suddenly got her full attention with one little phrase: ". . . when Ishtels ruled the world above . . ."

Laren was up on her elbows. "What? Ishtels ruled the world? What do you mean?"

He pulled himself up to face her. "It's in the Askirit tales."

She was as awake as if soldiers were upon them. "When? How? Is that all it says?"

"The wording of the legend is exactly this: 'Before the Maker judged the world—split it and scorched it—Ishtels ruled. Survivors of the cataclysm, trapped in Aliare's darkness, blamed them for the Maker's fury. In their bitterness, they blamed Ishtels for every misfortune, hunting and killing them everywhere. 'But hear this, you Askirit: the Maker judges all. Let every Ishtel face him—not your puny wrath.'"

Now it was Laren who was full of questions. How did they rule? How did they survive below? What more was known? Bren had few answers, only that the Askirit below had found ways around their own beliefs, persecuting them as the pagans did. "But up here, in the light, the Askirit are different—because of the story of Auret and the Ishtels."

"Story? Of Ishtels?" Laren had never heard of any story with an Ishtel in it.

"Of course you wouldn't. The Mazcaens hate stories about Auret. And this is the last one they'd let you hear."

"Tell it!"

Bren eased back, hands under his neck. He took his time, obviously enjoying her intensity. He slowly recited: "In the darkness of Aliare below, in a small Askirit village by the sea, villagers were angry. Fine knives with intricately carved bone handles were missing. An elder's personal ornaments had disappeared." Bren paused, looking up at her. "Understand, they had no light to see beautiful things, so they loved their carvings. Handles, pendants, sanctuary doors. They would love to run their fingers over a carving and sense the muscles in a bird's wing!"

"I know all that." She was still on her elbows, impatiently making out his expression in the starlight, urging him to continue.

"Some men found an Ishtel with his half-grown son not far from the village. They were dragged to the elders. The Ishtel had a well-carved knife, though none in the village could claim it. Yet they convinced themselves the Ishtels were guilty.

"Auret was a young man then. He heard they planned to give the Ishtels to sierent."

Laren grimaced. She knew well that meant leaving them outside for sierent's storms, which scoured the great hollows of the planet, destroying all in their path.

"Auret appeared among the villagers as they stood in a cavern; the Ishtels were on a narrow spit extending into the sea, blocked from shelter. As the winds started to gust, the villagers taunted them, ridiculing their terror.

"Auret said loudly, 'I know who really took the carvings.'

"An elder sneered at him, saying, 'How would you know?' for Auret was an outsider himself, having been washed up on their shores as a child.

"'Do you want the truth?' Auret asked.

"They ignored him as the winds increased.

"'Then I will take their place. The law demands you allow it.' And without waiting for a response, he commanded the Ishtel and his son to come into the cavern as he stepped out into the storm.

"Sierent sucked at the Ishtels' clothes, lifting their arms as they came. Auret said to them as they passed, 'I came to die for Ishtels.' Then Auret gripped his cane and limped his way slowly into the deadly storm."

"Cane?" Laren was suddenly pierced by a stab of recognition. "Why a cane?"

Bren cocked his head, wondering at the urgency in her voice. "Auret was crippled. When he'd first entered Aliare's darkness, they'd found him on shore crushed and nearly dead. Only a woman's prayers and constant care kept him alive."

Till now, all her thoughts had been on the Ishtels. Auret she had thought of as some Askirit god who did not concern her. But now she saw this Auret as clearly in her mind as she had in her dream. The cripple with the power, the purity. The man who loved Ishtels.

Bren said, "The ending is always told this way: The next morning Auret was seen in the crags, telling the Ishtel boy wonderful stories. Sierent had no power over him. And we are all Ishtels, you know. Like Auret, do not despise the off-scourings among you."

Laren was sitting up straight, her hand absently on her mouth, her eyes staring vacantly as she took in his remarkable words—words she could hardly imagine being said—and at the same time reliving every part of her dream.

"What's the matter?" Bren asked.

Should she tell him about the dream? It was intimate, personal, her dream to savor and feed on. Yet she also wanted to tell him and finally said, "I've seen him. I've seen the cripple!"

Bren looked perplexed. "But he's no longer a cripple. Queen Mela saw him healed and full of glory and power."

"Oh, he was full of power, and full of love. I saw him with Meleden, saw him as clear as ever I've seen you, his face all gouged and scarred but full of love."

Bren sat up beside her. "What are you talking about?"

"A dream. A dream as real as your hand."

She told him the details, unable to keep the words from tumbling out. "The rocks floating from my hands, and then shining ones making music with them—just like other dreams, all strange, but . . ."

"What makes dreams," Bren said, "and visions that seem to come from other worlds?" He began telling her for the first time the details of his experiences above the quake, and how the celestials had made him see everything so differently. "Peace and laughter in chaos. That's what it was."

Somehow it all seemed of a piece, and now she was hungry for stories of Auret. Bren told her one after another and tried to answer her many questions. It was nearly dawn before Bren ended up saying, "There's a teaching song from the Ishtel story—a song for children." He sang it quietly:

> *"If you see an Ishtel,*
> *You give that Ishtel hugs.*
> *If that Ishtel hugs you back,*
> *You say it's Auret's love."*

Bren squeezed Laren's arm. She liked the feel of his hand and was still filled with wonder. But she did not respond to his touch; she lay back and eased into sleep.

——— The Border ———

Galial was first up next morning. She called to them right away to get up and get going—every moment wasted increased their danger. Laren almost forced herself up, but then saw Bren hadn't moved. She fell dead asleep again until Galial's hiss in her ear. "Get up! Meleden's stirring."

Laren jerked herself upright, blinking and wobbling her head at the brightness. Whatever the meaning of last night's revelations, Galial's command had made her feel like less than a slave again.

All that day they followed deer trails, and she was too busy with Meleden and watching her feet to talk to Bren. He was probing ahead, looking in alarm at every noise. Galial kept whispering at Laren, as if upset at her, or just taking out her nervousness on an Ishtel.

Laren tried to digest all Bren had told her and how it connected to the dream. Sometimes she thought the dream was simply her imagination rising full blown from her extraordinary experiences. As she trudged warily through the forest, afraid of slipping and falling on Meleden and making her wail, she felt the same old sweat and fear, the same sense of being like a hunted deer. What, really, had changed? But her mind was a storm of new thoughts and questions.

Bren was getting anxious; they were close to Askirit territories, but he kept hearing suspicious sounds. Staying off the trails meant they were making slower progress and more noise. After talking with Laren most of the night, he knew he should feel total peace about their mission, but when a grouse flushed out of a pine in a loud explosion of feathers, his whole body shook.

Celestials can laugh in chaos, he thought. *Not me!*

He was so close to the border he decided to get back on a trail to make better time. But they had been hurrying along for only a short time when he heard what he thought was a man's voice.

No! Not when we're this close! His neck was prickling as he motioned his companions back into the woods. They scurried a considerable distance, then climbed up on a massive rock with trees growing all around it and with one tree growing up through a cleft in its middle.

"Maybe we can see something from up here," he whispered, getting everyone settled down on a patch of moss.

"Did you hear something?" Laren asked.

"Maybe."

Bren had just taken the baby from Laren when he heard a branch snap somewhere ahead. He squinted into the forest but saw nothing.

They heard more branches cracking underfoot, and then the sense of many men approaching. Bren strained for every sound and decided the men were parallel to the trail, on both sides of it, stalking anyone on it or near it.

Settling onto his back, he settled the baby on his chest, wishing they had gone deeper into the forest, wondering what the celestial beings who had laughed so confidently now thought about the terror soaking his body.

As the footsteps grew distinct under crunching leaves, only his head was raised a little on the knob of a thick trunk. Surely, he thought, they would suspect fugitives like them might be hiding on this high point. He clutched a piece of cheese and a cloth in case Meleden started making sounds, knowing he couldn't silence her but might comfort her just long enough. Just one cough, one whimper. . . .

Clearly, he and the women couldn't fight off this many. Just a few more moments, he prayed, as he matched his breathing to the quick breaths of the warm child on his chest.

As the soldiers slowly, slowly crunched toward them, the warm presence of Meleden on his chest and the thoughts of the celestials' always seeming near this strange baby began leaching out the terror. Even as the thick, squat men in bright multicolored uniforms came close, scanning the forest and making silent signs to each other, he felt the terror ebb, felt it being replaced by some peaceful presence. It was as if he could hear whispers from another world, assuring him that even if these soldiers with their wide blades and ugly purposes should spy them, nothing would stop the purposes that truly mattered. These feelings and thoughts were so incongruous as he watched the brightly woven jackets passing by that he patted Meleden with a drumming of his fingers on her back. As soon as he had done it, he realized how foolish it was, but his lips creased into what was almost a grin.

And then they were past them, the sounds and specks of color receding and disappearing among the trees.

None of them moved for a very long time.

Finally Laren reached out to touch Bren's hand, which lay on the baby's neck. She stroked it as she sometimes did to the child. He turned his head toward her. Black branches and a silvery cobweb behind her contrasted with her blue eyes and the light in her golden hair. Her delicate mouth puckered and threw a little kiss to the infant. She whispered something so quietly he could barely make it out.

"What?" he asked quietly.

"She's a wonder."

He traced Laren's small nose with his finger. "And so are you. Like a lily in the woods."

Her eyes darted to his, brows knotted. She did not look embarrassed nor pleased, but mystified.

He grinned. "But no lily ever had such exquisite freckles." Then his expression suddenly changed. "Laren, you're far more than a delicate flower; you're a spring birch—tenacious, tough, full of hidden strength. And you have the courage of an Enre!"

Her eyes were on the baby as she asked what an Enre was.

"Enre are Askirit women, chosen from birth. Elite warriors, magnificently trained. And they're deeply spiritual. Enre give up everything to follow the light, to fight for the kingdom."

Laren studied his face as she reached for Meleden, then took the baby into her arms. "I was chosen too. Chosen to grub for fish bones and rags."

Bren shook his head vigorously. "No—you were chosen to rescue Meleden!" He hopped down from the tree and helped Laren lower herself and the baby. "You were chosen to see kelerai with your own eyes and to walk in the light."

That evening they camped just over the border. At least Bren hoped only Askirit troops would patrol this close to Kelerai. They had circled far and come down along the sea, so the sounds of the waves were pleasant in Bren's ears. He had cut saplings for a lean-to, and now Galial was loading branches on the little roof. Laren had broken out the food and was talking to the baby, trying to get a response.

Bren leaned over the wide-eyed, wordless infant and made preposterous sounds, trying to coax a smile.

Laren laughed. "That won't do it. You'll just make her spit up." She tried to get a response by making soft, clicking sounds with her tongue.

What a delicate laugh Laren has, he thought. He told her he loved the sound of her laughter, that it was like waves on sand. Her eyes dropped again, and he reached over to lift her chin and make her look at him. "Your laughter is like music, but you think I'm lying."

Galial snapped a thick branch, threw it on the lean-to and asked irritably, "Food ready?"

Laren stood and hurriedly arranged the packets of dried food. They ate in silence, Bren thinking through what the morning would be like and what they would find in his own land. After the meal, he started walking toward the sea.

Galial got up and followed him. As soon as they were out of earshot, she grabbed his shoulder and turned him toward her. "What are you doing with that girl? Why are you staying up all night with her, telling her she's beautiful?"

He was amused by her fierce look and gave a little snort. She snorted back, as if his arrogance was intolerable. "You used that girl to get the baby. And now you want to mess with her." The big slave woman shuddered.

Bren shrugged away from her and walked to the edge of a hill above the sea. She matched him step for step, and as he looked down at the darkening water, she said bitterly from behind him, "Foolin' around with an Ishtel! Using her. Scum thing to do."

He spun around. "I've never taken the slightest advantage of Laren. Not once."

Her face broke into a disgusted sneer. "Maybe not. But you want to. It's obvious you want to, and that's what's disgusting!" She eyed him fiercely, her jaw hanging loose under bright ferret eyes.

Bren was dumbfounded. "How is that disgusting?"

She snapped her head back as if he were pretending he didn't know what she meant. "Ishtels must be with their own. You know that. Isn't it obvious? Doesn't nature itself show how inferior she is? White skin. Pale, deadly white. Like slugs and snake bellies and wriggling grubs."

He turned away from her and looked again at the sea. "Laren is the most beautiful woman I've ever seen."

Galial had spied a rotten tree trunk a short distance away and walked to it. She kicked at it hard again and again, breaking it into pieces, then with her knife probed in the crumbling, wet decay. Scooping something into her hand, she marched back to Bren. "What's beautiful?" She thrust her open palm in front of him; on it a curled white grub churned its many legs and rotated its little white head. "A bird is beautiful. A butterfly is beautiful. This—" and she thrust the grub under his nose—"this is not beautiful! It's only beautiful to a bird's beak."

Bren had nothing to say. Her eyes demanded a response, and when none came, her shaking jaw and mouth tried again to ram the obvious truth into him. "You tell Laren she's beautiful, but she sees through your lies. She knows what you want." She snapped her teeth in disgust. "How low do Askirit men sink just to get their way on a cold night?"

Geysers

Laren had heard it all. As Galial had followed Bren, she had clutched the sleeping Meleden in her arms and followed, sensing Galial wanted to talk alone with Bren. Ishtels survived by knowing as much as possible.

She had not been surprised at Galial's outrage, for the woman was obviously right. It was Bren who perplexed her. He had told her wonderful things and wonderful stories that had a ring of truth. Yet he also told her these lies about her being beautiful. Could anything he said be trusted, or was everything just a game to get her to give herself to him? He seemed unable to answer Galial.

Yet in the morning, as they strapped on their packs, Bren said heartily, "Laren, I've seen butterflies and I've seen birds. They're fine—but you're beautiful!" He said it with a laugh, so that she didn't know if he was teasing her or goading Galial. Or something else. How much could she trust Bren? How much of her new life was going to collapse on her?

She pushed the thoughts away, for as they entered the Askirit world, she must be alert. All her life she had feared the Askirit, and she couldn't trust Bren to be loyal to her.

At the outskirts of Kelerai, Bren led them to a high ridge where they could observe the great geysers erupt. Their rumblings shook the ground under Laren, making her fear a quake had begun, and then a wall of water and spray rose in the distance like a vertical sea.

Laren stared as it rose higher and higher, wind whipping spray in vast clouds off toward the mountains. "Notice the birds rising with it?" Bren said. "Look for rainbows—usually more than one."

"It's no wonder you worship it," Galial said.

"We don't worship kelerai. We worship the Maker, who made all the universe." Bren watched with them for a few more moments, then left to search for friendly forces.

Meleden was in Laren's arms. Was it her imagination or had the baby responded to these great rumblings and thunderings?

Her breathing and movements somehow seemed attuned to them. After all, from birth Meleden had felt and heard kelerai explode every morning.

Laren studied the child's face. What was going on in that mind of hers, which communicated no words and seemed to have no thoughts? Sitting here with Meleden, staring at the spray and massive geysers in the distance, Laren felt supremely grateful that she had been able to rescue the child. She felt Meleden herself somehow expressing gratitude, or those celestials Bren talked about whispering thanks.

The geysers were now a massive, steady spume, and she felt she could sit there watching it forever, sensing here all these strange things converging into a rising peace.

"I know that child!" It was a man's voice jarring Laren alert. "It's the royal babe, the one missing!" An old man, small and bent, stepped out from behind a tree and walked toward them. He studied the baby, then pronounced, "Sure is!" and scowled at the women. "You two don't look like you belong anywhere near here."

Laren wondered if Galial would strike the man before he could sound the alarm.

"We've brought the baby back," Laren said.

"Makes no difference." He shook his head mournfully. "The quakes are coming. The big ones. The ones that will shatter the world—shatter it like a fistful of shale under a hammer." He pointed at the great spouts in the distance. "Kelerai's bigger than ever— quakes are ripping the world apart. Royal babies? Nobody's going to be king or queen or prince or princess when they're sailing through space with chunks of rock whizzing by 'em." He said all this with a glum cheerfulness, as if the certainty of the fact and his own clear perception of it were the vital matters.

"Josk!" Bren's voice broke into the old man's warnings. "You've met my allies? Good. They took great risks to rescue Meleden. We must be taken quickly to the king."

The old man eyed him as if he had never seen him before. "There is no king. No queen either."

Bren started asking Josk questions, but the old man seemed to know little except that the world was about to be shattered. He said no soldiers had stayed around Kelerai, that they were all supposedly at the King's House in Aris, but that they may have fled from there too. Mazcaen raids had everyone terrified.

"Have there been any recently?"

Josk admitted none had occurred lately.

"That's because we stole their royal sacrifice," Bren said. "They must have thought that a bad omen for raids."

"Don't matter," Josk persisted. "World's going to blow apart anyway."

Part Two

*Love between man and woman
has created kingdoms and toppled them.
What a jester the Maker is!
What laughter we hear from beyond.*

—A VILLAGE SAYING

Chapter 5.

―――― Anarchy ――――

A soldier, two strange women, and a baby—even that unlikely troop roused fear on villagers' faces as the odd foursome traveled to Aris. Bren had retrieved his uniforms and gear at the deserted barracks at Kelerai; all military personnel had been summoned to the capital.

When they finally reached the city, they found Aris filled with soldiers and courtiers, but Mazcaen raids had paralyzed the capital. It didn't matter that the raids had stopped. No one had the courage to rule, so everyone with any power ruled a little, creating chaos by issuing conflicting commands to anyone who would obey. Bren remembered Gresen's hope that Varial and the Enre would take over, as a Varial generations ago had done when she had become queen. He sensed that elite corps of women could galvanize the nation if they stepped forward.

Searching in the turmoil of the city, Bren and the women spent a full day asking and dodging questions, all the time keeping the infant's face covered. Finally they located Bren's company on the bluffs overlooking the royal complex. A soldier pointed out Bren's captain hunched at the bluff's edge, staring down at the soaring slabs of stone making up the walls of the King's House.

Bren strode up to him and came smartly to attention, slapping his hand against his scabbard in the expected manner.

The captain stood, slowly turned, then looked him up and down. Bren wondered by his dispirited look if he even recognized him. When the captain finally asked, "What did you learn?" The older man sounded as if he were inquiring about field supplies.

"The Mazcaens had the royal child." Bren motioned toward the two women. "We brought Meleden back."

The captain's face finally flickered with interest. He followed Bren to where Laren held the baby and watched as Bren pulled back the covering. "How did you get her?"

"The young woman helped. She didn't want the baby sacrificed."

The captain shrugged. "Won't matter much." His sagging face had lost all military bearing. "The way it's going, the Mazcaens will soon have all of us trussed up on their altars."

"I heard the king—"

"Was almost captured. Fell on his own sword so he wouldn't be taken. Wasn't king for more than four days. Now, nobody wants to be king." The captain hunched his shoulders as if a heavy pack rested on them.

"What about the Enre? What about Varial?"

"They say it's not their time."

Bren knitted his brows. For a while he stared at the city below and the slopes on the sides, then turned to look behind them. "Why is the entire company bunched near the lip of the bluff?"

The officer grimaced and took a long, deep breath. "We're guarding the King's House." He swept his arm across the horizon. "Supposedly this is the right place to spot raiders. Yesterday they spread us out in a thin line—as if royals know anything about strategy! They shiver down there like rabbits waiting for weasels—always talking about Mazcaens torturing people like them. So they've deployed the entire Askirit army to protect them." He spat over the bluff at the King's House far below. "But that won't protect them in the least—not after we lose the whole country."

Stepping closer to Laren, Bren gently took Meleden from her and held the baby chest-high in front of his captain. "Isn't this a sign?" he asked. "Here's the queen's daughter, the sacrifice to empower the Mazcaens against us. And she rests in our arms." He nodded toward Galial and Laren. "And aren't they signs? They who fled such desecrations? Think! We have the light. We have all the glories of the past and all the promises. We have the sure knowledge that Auret has visited us and helps us face even the enormities ranged against us."

Bren tucked Meleden under his left arm and reached out with his right to grip his captain's elbow, the sign in the rituals to remember the past. "How is it that everyone has forgotten: 'The light is always greater than the darkness.'"

The captain's jaw had lifted a little. He reached out and, as Bren had, gripped the elbow wedged against the bundled baby. "You don't have to convince me. You must convince those whose mouths are so large and whose hearts are so timid."

Slippery Bodies

Young voices shouting and screaming made Laren wince as she followed Bren into a big cavern. She felt disoriented by the commotion of many children splashing and jumping in the natural pools. Even after they joined the smallest children in the smallest pool, she felt threatened by so much noise that might suddenly surprise her with a confrontation.

Eyes on the ground, Meleden in her arms, she glanced up now and then in the Ishtel way for unnoticed glimpses. She couldn't understand how they were letting an Ishtel among these royal children. One furtive glance showed a big boy of about fourteen staring at her. She moved closer to the small children and was relieved to hear him plunge back into the water.

Holding the baby gave her a trickle of peace, some reason for being in this strange place, for staying alive. But she was alarmed that even this one hope might be taken from her. Bren was here to search out the child's old nurse. When he found her, what place would be left for Laren?

Through the commotion of skinny, wet bodies chasing and skidding on the smooth rocks she noticed women posted around the pools, obviously ready to rescue. Occasionally they called out reproofs, but the words were like whispers cast into the din.

Galial tossed back her head and shook her thick hair. "These children sure aren't worried about raids."

"I wouldn't want to be in charge of them," Laren said. "What if one drowned?"

She watched Bren approach an old woman tending two little boys. On seeing him, she quickly reached up for his hand and pulled herself up, welcome written large on her wrinkled face. The woman had a regal bearing; certainly she was no slave.

Bren pointed at Laren, and she realized she had been watching them brazenly. Her face went hot, and she looked down at her feet as they approached.

They greeted her, and the old woman's hand moved Meleden's blanket. Laren glanced furtively upward and saw the old, runed face alight, as if an old field of cracked and crumbling furrows had suddenly become golden, shimmering wheat. Gresen gathered the baby into her old arms, saying, "Welcome home, child."

Laren felt as if some part of her had been cut from her body. She watched the woman's lips pursed in a web of wrinkles. "Prayers night and day for you," she was murmuring through tears.

"Your prayers brought her here," Bren said.

"I fought the images in my head of bloody sacrifices."

Bren put his hand on the child's forehead. "They had chosen her. But this young woman, Laren, would not let it happen."

Gresen turned and looked at her, but Laren did not look up. "How?"

"She's remarkable!" he said, boldly touching her golden hair.

"Mazcaen?"

Bren grinned. "No. But a royal. A royal Ishtel!"

Laren blushed at his absurd irony. She longed to bolt away. Was Bren cruel, or did the Askirit joke among themselves like this? She glanced at Galial; her expression was pinched and cold.

"She carried Meleden out in a slop bucket," Bren said. "Right past the guards, right past the crowds in the market!"

Laren felt something touching her elbow; with her free arm the old woman was encircling her in an embrace. Gresen still held the baby so that the little form was pressed between them. "May the Maker bless you beyond all imaginings!" The old woman released her, then cupped Laren's lowered chin and lifted it so that she was compelled to look into her face. "We are all enormously grateful."

The warmth of Gresen's body lingered. Laren had not felt a woman's touch for many years, and never with such enormous affirmation. She longed to sense this connection and wholeness forever.

"You are the most blessed woman in all the kingdom," Gresen said. "You've brought us hope, and the love we so sorely missed."

The Dais of Light

The King's House was not a house at all but a magnificent palace soaring from the rocky plains like the sea cliffs surrounding it. Light was the theme, for their ancestors had come from the darkness below. Askirit music, clothing, architecture, all used symbols of light. The Great Hall with its open chambers reached up and drew down shafts of light into the corridors. Under the regal dais, the broadest shafts of all streamed down from the highest apex.

But no king sat under that light. Instead of orderly process and guards in place, royal relatives and courtiers milled around with drinks in their hands and sour apathy on their faces. Bren and the captain, with the three women and the infant, entered like beggars at a fair. The captain ambled slowly in, looking around, studying faces. "We need to introduce you to someone," he said to Bren.

"You should do the talking, Captain. You have some rank."

"But you rescued the child. And you have the vision."

Yes, Bren thought, he had seen things other men had not. He asked, "Among everyone here, who has the most rank and wisdom and courage?"

The captain's glance swept through the hall, and then he laughed. "Rank? Plenty have rank!" Then he nodded toward a frail, lanky man sitting alone on an aisle bench, oblivious to the noise, staring straight ahead at the light striking the dais. "But to find a little rank and much wisdom and courage, there is old Tatt."

They approached the man, and as soon as the captain spoke, Tatt insisted on gripping his cane and rising. His right arm and the side of his face above it shook in a constant tremor, but his greeting was strong and warm. Beneath his thick white hair and eyebrows, a convergence of veins on his jaw joined in a tangled red blotch.

The captain locked his fingers in a military salute. "I sent this soldier to scout the Mazcaens. Instead, he penetrated Belez and rescued the queen's child." He nodded toward Meleden in Laren's arms.

The old man's head turned, and he stepped closer to the strange young woman. He looked down at the infant for a long time, then looked up at the three women: the old Askirit nurse, the big, resolute slave, the small, fair Ishtel. He nodded to Gresen. "How happy this must be for you."

Gresen nodded back. "None of us dared hope for this."

Tatt turned to the captain. "And what now?"

The captain shrugged and shifted his eyes toward Bren. The old man followed his eyes and appraised the young man who had done such a remarkable thing. "And what now?" he repeated.

"Now is our chance," Bren said without hesitation. He chopped the air with his hand like a blade. "Why are we so frightened of the Mazcaens? The Maker—he who teaches our fingers to war—the Maker hates their butchery! What now?" Bren turned his head as if amazed at the question. "We must seek the light, and we must grasp the sword. We must cry out for the power of the righteous. It wasn't I who rescued the child, but the ones who watch over her."

The old man studied Bren, his thin lips raised at the corners, making the red splotch partially disappear behind the folds of his skin. Holding the top of the bench, he raised his cane in the air and waved it in a circle to get someone's attention. Bren followed his eyes and saw a woman standing by the wall, a strong, alert young woman. Enre, he concluded. When she noticed Tatt, she came over to him immediately, and he whispered something to her.

The Enre walked briskly away. Tatt turned to Bren. "Come, then. You must tell the people." He started off down the long aisle toward the dais, not looking behind him, pacing himself with his cane straight to his target. The little troop with the good news to announce followed him at his slow pace.

When he reached the dais, Tatt turned to ask for Bren's help up the walkway. Once on the platform, standing with his cane under the convergence of light, he asked the captain to call for attention. He did so with the booming voice that Bren remembered well from the parade grounds.

When all eyes finally looked toward them Tatt said as loudly as he could, "Listen! This soldier has shown Mazcaens are not invincible. Far from it!" He clapped his hand on Bren's shoulder. "Alone, he entered their capital, and just before they could sacrifice our royal child, he stole her away! Stole her from the dark bowels of their temple! Right in the heart of Belez." Tatt made a wide sweeping motion toward the three women. "And here is the child!"

The great hall buzzed; people crowded forward to get a look at the baby. Tatt shouted over the noise, "We thought Meleden was dead, but here she is alive, bringing us hope."

The old man watched them pressing forward, talking heatedly. Bren noticed the Enre re-enter the hall with a tall woman who marched straight to the dais. As she stepped onto it, Tatt welcomed her and introduced her to Bren as Varial, leader of all the

Enre. She thanked Bren for his successful mission by gripping his wrist with three fingers, the sign of exceptional valor.

The Enre were uniquely trained warriors, deeply religious, and this woman who led them all looked as if she could lead the nation as well. Bren asked, "Shouldn't you and the Enre lead us— now, when we have the chance for victory?"

She smiled, chin raised, head cocked just slightly, as if to decide if he were attempting flattery or genuinely asking. "It is not our time," she said. "We have other tasks just as pivotal to the Maker's plans." Her eyes sparkled and her mouth was lifted in humor as she said that, and Bren was reminded of the lighthearted-edness of the celestials, and he smiled with her.

Tatt banged his cane on the floor to get attention. "Listen, all of you, to Bren, the queen's soldier. I have listened to him, and I have asked him to speak, for he sees what all of us should see."

Bren looked out at the royal faces, angry with them all for their spinelessness. "When I escaped from Belez, I was dumb-founded at what awaited me here in Aris—people cowering like rabbits." He was unafraid of what they thought as he demanded, "Do you think Auret forgot us? Has the light blinked out in the world? Hah!" He pointed down at the child. "This wondrous baby the Mazcaens would have sacrificed to empower their raids against us, this child is the Maker's sign!"

He paused and stepped back, thinking Tatt would take over, but the old man kept looking at him expectantly. Bren turned back to face the packed hall, for word had spread about the baby, and people were coming in every door and packing the corridors. "Were our queen alive, she would take heart! Mela would say that the quakes were signs. That we who seek the light must take heart, for the Maker delights in holy courage, but he turns away when we grovel."

Bren hadn't meant to get quite so pointed; he was shaking as he stepped back to let the old man speak again.

The people were so quiet Tatt's response was easily heard all over the Great Hall. "I'm told I have a little wisdom from all my years." He smiled broadly and the red splotch for a moment completely disappeared. "I'm wise enough to know we need someone to lead us. Some of us are too old, others too fearful. Varial's mission is elsewhere. But look at the fire in this young warrior. He has the anointing! He has proven his mettle." Tatt let a long silence reign over the great crowd. Then he said, "Choose the soldier. Choose the one who has brought us hope!"

The hall turned into a cacophony of spirited discourse, and Bren was flabbergasted. He had not thought of this happening at all. He was not even an officer, not even a full-blooded Askirit.

After a time, Tatt had the captain call the assembly to order again. "I hear some of you saying Bren is not of royal blood." Tatt lifted his cane and struck it hard against the dais. "He is a soldier of the queen! How did Yosha and Asel form the kingdom? By royal blood? No, by courage and vision."

Here and there across the hall, Bren heard his name being repeated. He heard it being chanted in the front and then louder and louder until the entire Great Hall reverberated with "Bren, Bren, Bren." Yet he felt no elation, merely amazement. He felt as if he were watching all this with holy amusement from above the mountains and, in watching, felt a growing sense of duty and certitude. This, apparently, was why he was still alive in this collapsing world.

The chanting kept going on, as if the people at last had found something to shout that could lift their whimpering spirits and expiate their guilt. Tatt stood beside Bren with one hand on his cane, the other raised with open palm to the light above.

Bren raised his arms for silence. When the hall quieted he said, "You must know something else. Do you see the beautiful young woman holding the child?" He held his hand out toward Laren. "She is an Ishtel, despised by the Mazcaens, lower than the lowest slave. Yet she struck out against the darkness; she carried the little princess right past the guards, knowing the unspeakable would happen if she were caught."

He motioned for her to join him; Gresen took the baby from her and pushed Laren toward the little ramp. He stepped down toward her, took her hand and led her up to where the light streamed brightly on her golden hair and delicate skin and features. Bren heard gasps from people seeing her for the first time.

She's lovely, he thought, *more lovely than she can possibly know.*

Golden Hair

One moment Laren had been standing with the warm baby in her arms beside Gresen and Galial, secure in their presence and the baby's warmth. Then she was up there alone, in full view of all those hungry eyes, she who all her life had cowered under even one person's stare. Their gasps and their whispers at her peculiarities humiliated her, but she kept her head erect and eyes off the ground, for Bren had told her she must do so here in the Great Hall.

Then came the worst of all. People excitedly climbed up the dais. She was separated from Bren, surrounded by alien, cultured beings, forced to respond to inquisitive eyes and aristocratic mouths. They wanted to know every detail about the rescue.

"How did you put that huge baby in a bucket?" a woman asked.

"She fit fine."

"But how could you carry the bucket past the guards? You're so little."

Laren remembered the captain saying these royals were shaking like rabbits waiting for weasels, but these seemed painfully self-assured.

"What do you eat in Belez?" another woman asked. She was chewing on something and obviously never lacked for food.

I ate garbage, Laren thought, but she replied, "Corn and meat."

They're playing with me, she shouted inside herself, *playing with me like nasty boys with a fly. Pull off a wing, poke, and inspect—touching my hair.* She saw their eyes keep shifting to it, following its tumbling past her cheeks and over her shoulders, for there was not a head like hers among them.

She heard Bren somewhere talking, surrounded by adulation, his tone confident and urgent. If only Meleden were in her arms, but she stood alone, the ordeal going on and on, her mouth dry with mumbling.

Finally, Bren rejoined her and they stepped down. She looked everywhere for Galial and Gresen, but all she saw was the rapidly emptying hall. As the two of them walked down the main aisle, six soldiers on each side kept pace with them. Even Bren's captain now walked behind them, guarding the new hope for the nation.

As they stepped out into the evening shadows she whispered to Bren, "I'm sorry. I'm sorry."

He stopped and cocked his head quizzically. "For what?"

He hadn't heard her shameful mumblings, she thought. He hadn't seen that her eyes simply couldn't keep looking at those cultured, confident people. "I said stupid things. I couldn't look at them." She stared down at his stout military boots opposite her ragged moccasins.

"They loved you!" he exclaimed. "They kept coming to me after talking to you, and they loved your humble way, your shy smile." Once more he forced her chin upward, just when she thought she could rest her eyes on the ground. "Every one of them thought you were a princess. I've said to you again and again that you're lovely, and now everyone compares you to little flowers and songbirds."

How could he say such things? she thought bitterly. The lovely garbage girl, princess of the slop bucket. Why keep twisting the knife?

They hiked to where they had camped, and at last she could hear Galial's voice and saw Gresen in the distance. She longed to rush to them and to hold Meleden, but Bren stopped and waved away the soldiers. He led her to the base of a tree, then gripped her by the shoulders as one does a comrade after success in war. "How can I make you understand? Here, you're not a despised Ishtel. You're beloved!" He let go her shoulders and then gently encircled her with one arm. "If Gresen can say thank you, then I can too." He put his other arm around her and held her as tightly as Gresen had, but she felt numb, mystified, discordant.

He released her, took her hand, and led her to the cliffs overlooking the sea. They sat down and listened to its waves striking the shore below.

"I will be made king, you know."

"I know."

"You made that possible."

The night sounds near the sea were not that different from the river sounds where she had always lived. A few unfamiliar birds, louder waves, but the same insects, the same constellations above. She looked and listened in silence, soothed by familiarity. Finally she asked, "What will being king mean for you? Does a king of the Askirit go to war?"

He was chewing on a stalk of hay and spat it out. "They're counting on it."

Laren smiled and nodded.

She felt his fingers on her cheek, dancing lightly as if communicating a message, moving over her face in a circle. Then he brought his own face close to hers and, strangely, fluttered his eyelashes against her skin as he pressed a small object into her hand. "You don't understand these messages, but an Askirit girl would."

Bren tapped another strange dance on her wrist. "We have a whole language of touch called Yette. My fingers on your face said, 'You are more lovely than you can imagine.' My eyelashes on your skin said the guardians of my eyes will always keep them directed at you alone. And the carving in your hand is of two birds. Wedding birds, for they mate for life."

He put both his hands over hers, squeezing the carving against her palm, then released her. "A girl among us who receives such a carving knows she has received a solemn request."

Laren ran her fingertips over the wings of the birds in her hand. They were interlocked, wrapped together forever on a small piece of wood.

"You've been touched by love of the child. You share my love for the light, and you disdain the dark. The Maker's spirit is in you."

The wood felt weighty in her hand, as if it were too heavy for her little palm.

"Do you know what I am saying? I'm asking that you be my queen."

The preposterous words dripped onto her like hot wax from a candle. She was glad Galial was not near enough to hear all this.

She felt she would have to say yes. Did she have any other choice? But it would mean a lifetime of ordeals like the one she had just endured on the dais, a different sort of sacrifice on an Askirit altar.

She handed the carving back. "You and your people have strange eyes, to call beautiful my colorless face, with a slit for a mouth."

He smiled. "The Maker made you much different from us, and he thinks you're beautiful."

She refused to be drawn into his banter. "It doesn't matter." Her voice was flat and resigned. "Just don't separate me from Meleden."

Bren suddenly stood. "Laren, I'm not ordering you to do this!" His voice had taken on an edge. "I'm offering you a sharing of the challenges we talked about on the trail. We have experienced so much together. I'm offering you my loyalty. But if you find me ugly—"

"No," she said, standing up beside him, alarmed at his tone. "You're the beautiful one."

She had said it simply, with no sarcasm meant, but he snapped back, "Do you mean I'm vain?"

She laughed, but without humor. "You have full lips and rich skin and wide, dark eyes. A stallion is beautiful; you are beautiful. But it doesn't matter."

Bren put one arm around her. "No. It doesn't matter."

He pressed the carving back into her hand. "Sleep with the birds in your hand tonight. Maybe you will come to think them beautiful too."

Ceremonies

The Great Hall of the King's House was already full of celebrants when Bren looked in. The word had spread everywhere that he would be made king today, and all eyes were toward the rear of the main aisle, where they expected the procession to begin. But Bren was at a side entrance, determined in this quickly arranged ceremony to bend tradition to his own purposes. He had not ridden here on a royal horse with trumpets blaring. Instead of wearing thick robes with rustling sleeves, he was dressed as a soldier. With a nod to the priests and dignitaries behind him, he suddenly strode briskly across the front and mounted the dais.

The high priest followed, then turned to address the people. "We are here to proclaim a king of the Askirit, a king who seeks the light!" He stepped back and Varial walked to Bren and put both hands on his head, pronouncing a blessing. Then he was left alone at the front.

His eyes swept back and forth over the assembly. "I haven't come to you with horses and trumpets and rustling sleeves." He raised his right arm high and turned the long sword in his hand back and forth so that the midday light streaming down reflected from it, sending glints dancing among the congregants. "We are at war. Like Yosha and Asel on the run when they founded the kingdom, we will have simple ceremonies. We will take no time for festivals or feasts, for we must quickly turn to hard duties."

He paused for an uncomfortably long time, then asked, "Are you ready for that?"

Bren didn't care that he, a common soldier, was berating the Askirit nobility. He thought only of his passion to convey his vision, to ignite that passion among the people. "Who are these Mazcaens who have terrified Aris? When they came up out of darkness with our ancestors, they claimed to love the light. But now they have embraced the worst evils of darkness."

He motioned for Galial to join him and the big former slave climbed the ramp. He put his hand on her shoulder. "See this woman? Galial was a Mazcaen slave, and she took courage from the innocent child. We Askirit must repent of many sins, but we do not make slaves of men and women the Maker has made."

He held them steady in his gaze. "Do you still believe the light is greater than the darkness?"

At his nod, Laren then ascended with Meleden in her arms. "Who are these Mazcaens, that they would butcher this mute child to appease their gods?" He held the child aloft. "Laren

He handed the child to Galial, then took Laren's hand. As he touched her, he caught a responded to the light and snatched the child from death. Now is the time for every one of you to share her courage."whiff of ele, the bride scent. When he had gone to her that morning, she had been very quiet. But she had kept her eyes on his when she said, "The birds are beautiful."

She had said it as if mentioning the time of day, then had looked down. He had tried to talk more, but he had been urged away by those making preparations.

Bren was tracing his fingers over her wrist in a message as he proclaimed to all the people, "You must know one more thing. If you will make me king, you will also make Laren queen, for first, we will be wed."

Laren heard whispers roll through the great hall and then turn into a staccato, rhythmic banging of feet. She turned her eyes to the front wall to avoid seeing the people making those angry sounds. But Bren was swinging his and her hands to the rhythm, and when he saw her distraught look said, "It's traditional at weddings. Look at their joyous faces!"

She would not look at their faces, but she did glance at his. Melne, the bold, astringent groom's scent, was distinct in the air. She hated the way her dress exposed her shoulders; she wanted to hide her face, wanted veils covering it. She longed to wash off the markings the women had applied to accentuate her eyebrows and enhance her lips.

But she had decided on this. She had decided that the hope she had found in the child and the love Bren had for her was somehow all mixed together and that she couldn't cast it all aside. She would seek the light Bren always talked about.

The priest was asking them questions, and then he was placing a small bird into her hands. She looked across at Bren; he too held a small, quivering bundle of feathers. He smiled at her, then reached out, handing his male bird to her while holding out his other hand for the female. It nearly escaped as she gave it to him.

At the priest's instructions, they pledged their eternal, holy love. Then, with arms uplifted, they opened their hands to release the birds. The yellow markings on their blue wings flashed brightly as they flew up in the sun's rays and quickly found their way out.

Bren embraced her, his hands splayed wide and strong across her shoulder blades. "You will grow in love," he whispered.

Someone put on Bren the required gown with its rustling, ridged sleeves, and then the high priest was draping a chain over his head so that the ancient Askirit pectoral hung on his chest. "Touch its sharp edges," said the high priest.

He ran his fingers over the carving of serrated wings rising, with rays of light at the top. It made little cuts in his fingertips. "Uphold the cutting edge of the law, even when it divides your own flesh," the priest commanded. "Even when it destroys those you love. But remember also the wings. The wings of hope."

Varial hung on him the pendant made for Queen Mela. It depicted a burst of light from a dark center, flames rising and curling. "Remember your holy trust," she said. "Rule for the Maker's glory, not your own."

—— First Night ——

Rich brocades hung everywhere in the huge room. A servant entered to take away the ample tray of food Laren had been unable to finish. "Leave it for now," she said, unable to let good food out of her sight.

After the ceremony they had whisked her to this complex of adjoining rooms in the King's House where women fussed over her and asked about her every whim. They made many sly comments about the night ahead and fussed with all sorts of preparations she didn't understand. At Laren's request they had brought Galial and Gresen and the baby to her, and they had spent the rest of the afternoon together. But then the women asked them to leave as they smiled and winked and said the king would soon come.

But Laren was not at all sure of that; Bren was off planning military strategy, meeting with advisors, perhaps working through the night. She felt foolish waiting in this fancy dressing gown they had put on her, staring at the cut flowers in every corner.

Then she heard a commotion in the hall and Bren's voice taking leave of other men and his heavy boots sounding in the next room. Another moment and he entered softly, boots gone, looking weary but with a smile on his face. He came to her and lightly, formally embraced her.

"The officers are magnificent. They don't need new strategies—just someone to coordinate and inspire!" He sat down on a chair and undid his jacket. "I hope you're all right. Did they bring Meleden to you?"

"They do everything for me." She sat down on a chair opposite him. "I wonder if they'll start putting the food in my mouth."

He laughed. "I'm not used to it either. No one ever waits on a soldier—but everyone falls all over a king." He reached over to the food and picked up a thick wedge of bread and a clump of berries. "I'm tired."

He stood and removed his jacket. She stared at the floor, and he reached down for her chin.

"Don't do that."

"Oh?" He backed away. "It's the only way you'll ever look at me."

"But I can't become an Askirit in one day. It's natural for an Ishtel's eyes to look down—but you're always grabbing my chin and lifting my face."

He took a long, deep breath, said he was sorry, then tossed his jacket into a corner.

She walked over, picked it up, and carefully draped it over a chair. "I have no right to complain."

"Complain all you want," he said cheerfully. He finished the little meal, then stood, took her hands, and pulled her up to his embrace. "We both have to learn and change. But not too much! Don't lose your shyness."

He held the tray out to her. "It's customary, you know, for an Askirit bride to prepare for the wedding night, to gather soft rushes and pile them up and to choose the scents. What are the customs among the Ishtels?"

She ignored his question, for there was no Ishtel custom, none at all. She said simply, "Your women have prepared me well." She took a few steps to an open doorway and motioned toward the great pile of rushes and flowers laid in the corner. She picked up several little scent bags on a small side table. "I couldn't choose among them," she said, handing them to him.

"You don't need any scent at all." He nuzzled her neck. "Just the natural scent of Laren."

She stepped back, wondering what he meant, then asked, "The scent of the garbage girl?" She attempted to laugh, but it came out like a little squeak. Embarrassed, she lifted toward him the ringlets of hair by her cheeks. "You're supposed to tie the scent strips on these. They did all sorts of things to my hair, to make me beautiful."

Bren ignored the hint of sarcasm. "You were beautiful on the dais this morning, with the sun streaming on your loose hair. And you're beautiful here, with ringlets of gold around your face."

Crazy, fancy words. She knew her yellow hair and washed-out face. She wondered if Bren thought green was purple or up was down. But she wouldn't argue with him as he put his arms around her, pulling her tighter. She stood impassive, head lowered.

Bren's arms were trembling. "You have no idea, do you, Laren, the power a woman has over a man?" He turned to pick up the tiny strips of cloth. "Especially a young, inexperienced man." He squeezed a drop of scent on each of the little strips, then began fumbling in her hair to tie them on, as was the custom.

Men always have their way, she thought. *They take their pleasure and the woman bloats up and waits for the pains of birth.* Laren was shaking a little herself.

"I won't hurt you." He held her at arm's length and tried to look into her eyes, but they were lowered again. She waited for his hand to pull her chin higher, but instead he moved away.

"I won't touch you until you want me to."

Laren felt the same as she had on the garbage dumps when Ishtel men kept after her. But she had decided to accept this remarkable man—it was all said and done—so she said, "I came of my own free will. I know I'm yours. Do with me as you choose."

A little groan escaped from him. "I'll not have you that way. That's not the Laren I long for." He sat down and fingered the few berries remaining on the tray, poking them back and forth, looking away from her.

"It's all right," she said. She did not want him angry, she did not want to be cast out.

He absently flicked the berries from side to side, lips pressed tightly together. He got up, scooped the scents off the little table and put them all on the floor by the door.

She objected, "You don't have to . . ."

He turned to her again. "Do you know how the Askirit courted below?" He touched her face with the fingertips of both his hands. "In the darkness, they would touch each others' faces. They would trace each contour of cheeks and forehead and nose and chin. And if a young woman cared at all for a young man, she would lightly graze her lips across his." He rippled his fingers across her lips as lightly as flower petals. "It was the sign of the beginnings of affection."

He took her in his arms again. "We haven't courted. Maybe we need to." He pressed her hand against his face. "I'm not the one to graze your lips with mine. That's the woman's choice—to give that little sign that someday love might grow."

Laren didn't hesitate. She stretched upward and Bren bent down; with her hand on his cheek, she grazed his rich, full lips with her thin, flat ones.

She thought he would then carry her to the pile of rushes. But Bren said, "The sign of emerging affection. A man is supposed to take hope from that." And he squeezed both her hands and quietly slipped away.

Chapter 6.

—— Skills from the Past ——

"Whoop!" The shout echoed all through the Great Hall and into the officers' planning room, where Bren was startled in mid-speech. Then came a hubbub of thuds and scrapings and children's voices.

"The troops you ordered, sir," said an officer with a grin.

Bren smiled back. "The lame, the blind, the deaf. . . ."

In the great hall they watched the gaggle of once-evicted children returning to the home the queen long ago had given them. Bren was glad his promise to Gresen was being enacted so quickly, despite the risks of alienating the royal squatters.

A bald old man in an ancient shirt and pants let out another whoop as he scurried among the blind, herding them toward the dais, tapping messages on their arms and wrists, making strange sounds through his teeth and with his fingers.

"They refer to him as the 'White Whirlwind.'" The officer chuckled. "Used to have white hair. Named Leas. Lots older than he looks. Indefatigable. Eccentric. Full of crazy ideas."

Leas. Bren recognized the name. He had been the mentor of Queen Mela, the fanatic keeper of all the old lore from their ancestors below.

Other groups of children with various deformities came behind Leas and the blind children. Soon they had filled the dais, children of all ages, and were encircling it ten deep. The bright noon light streamed down on them as they knelt and recited prayers from the liturgy. Bren could hear the voice of Leas leading them:

> *We are stunned each day by your wonders.*
> *By the roar of water and the hiss of steam.*
> *But the greatest wonder, Maker of worlds,*
> *The greatest wonder is your love for us.*

The little ceremony was quickly over, the feeble-minded and smallest children already wandering off around the edges. Leas was busily bustling among his charges, directing them to their assigned quarters, when he looked up to see Bren in front of him.

"The king!" Leas slapped his knuckles against his palm several times in an ancient, loud salute Bren had never heard before. The old man's face was alight. "Queen Mela must be smiling down on you." His bald head bobbed as he talked, and he wore a thick belt of pouches around his middle with contraptions dangling that swayed as he moved. "Good riddance to those whining royals," Leas said bluntly.

"They'll have to prove their royalty in battle," Bren responded, "not by lounging here."

He walked down the corridor with Leas who said, "We're grateful you've let the children back."

"Plenty of room for both children and the work of the kingdom."

Leas ushered the blind boys into a large room while directing the girls down the hall. "You may find that helping the children will help you to save the kingdom." He gave Bren an enormous wink, his bald head cocked at a sharp angle, then pulled off his big, pouched belt and handed it to him.

Bren hefted it and shook it a little so it jangled.

"Don't you know what it is?" The man's eyes were big with amazement at Bren's puzzled expression.

"Of course. Keitr belt." Everyone knew their ancestors had filled such pouches with poisonous, bat-like creatures and launched them in the darkness against their enemies.

Leas looked at his young king with a knowing smile, saying nothing.

Bren said, "No one has ever found keitr up here."

The smile beneath the bald pate grew broader. "Maybe not. Then again . . ." Leas pulled him farther down the hall and into a small room, then closed the door behind them.

"You haven't found keitr, have you?" Bren demanded. "If you have—"

"See! See how it intrigues you?" He took the belt from Bren and replaced it on his hips. "Listen, the Mazcaens always attack at night, terrifying our people. They use the night, sowing panic. Just like our ancestors did down there with keitr."

Leas carefully opened a pouch, pulling out an inner sleeve bulging with something that began squirming in his hand. "The Mazcaens don't know we haven't found keitr, just as you weren't sure. And in the night, when they attack, we can make them think we have."

Bren felt foolish listening to the old eccentric. The officers would probably laugh at him if they knew he was in here talking about keitr. He didn't know if he should continue the conversation at all, but he said, "All the techniques of launching them, of—"

"Techniques?" Leas was moving his fingers as if yanking out a keitr and poising to launch it. "All my life I've studied the techniques. I've taught my blind boys every trick year after year after year. We know how to launch them in the dark, how to coordinate them with wide sheaves of spears."

Bren could see why they called him the White Whirlwind. His hands were in fast motion, his head bouncing as he talked. "What is it in your hand?" Bren demanded.

"A bat. Just a simple bat. But come outside with me tonight, and I'll show you how we can make the Mazcaens think it's keitr striking. And I have scores of blind young men trained in Old Askirit skills. They're ready for the night raids of the enemy."

Mysteries

The crippled boy, about six, had pestered Laren and Gresenincessantly about going down to the sea near their rocky enclave. He was with them to help with the infants. He held Meleden for a few moments, then they sent him to rescue a little maimed girl when she got stuck between rocks, and again when she cried after slipping in a pool. But mostly he chattered about the waves and the shells down there and why couldn't they go and when would they go, and the feeble-minded boy started chiming in.

"I'll take them down," Gresensaid. "You stay with Meleden."

Laren was grateful. Gresenknew the Ishtel didn't like watching children on the shore, worrying when they disappeared in the water, baking under the sun and slapping at flies. She also knew Laren liked to be alone with Meleden. She had no significant duties as Queen, just, it seemed, staying out of everyone's way, with Bren long gone defending the kingdom.

She watched them descend, a toddling deaf boy holding the old woman's hand, the blind boy just ahead carrying the little maimed girl. Her whole one side had been mangled in some accident; to get somewhere she had to crawl or be carried.

Meleden had been uncomfortable all morning. Laren picked her up and put her head on her shoulder, but she squirmed and then began to fuss. The infant acted as if she couldn't get enough air. Laren hiked her up high on her shoulder and patted her back, but it made her fuss even more. She began gasping, making a thick, wheezing sound every time she tried to suck in air.

Gresenand the children were now little figures on the sea's edge, and Laren began to wish they hadn't left. Gresenhad so much more experience. Meleden was getting more and more restless; what if she died? Laren knew the child was often close to it, every infection hitting her harder than other children. She loved to be alone with Meleden, to watch her and hold her, but she didn't want to be alone with her when she died.

Her breathing became even more labored. Laren opened the child's mouth and tried to clear away obstructions, but Meleden just squirmed and moaned and perspired heavily. Her face was flushed and her legs began kicking.

Should she call out for Gresen? How could this be happening, when she had gone to such risk to save the child? What should she do to help her? The presences she had so often sensed protecting her seemed to have fled. She couldn't even hold Meleden close now, only lightly on her lap because her head was swinging back and forth, as if she was desperately trying to find relief.

Maker, where are you? Laren's mind was full of promises and prayers she had been learning among these Askirit, but here was Meleden dying on her lap and what difference did all those words mean? Yet she silently called out to the Maker, prayed all the prayers she could remember. Her face became as wet and flushed as the child's as she helplessly stroked the baby's hot cheeks.

"She looks very bad." The voice was Varial's, and Laren's first thought was that she had heard her praying, but then realized she had said nothing aloud.

"I don't know what to do for her."

"We can pray." Varial sat beside her, looking down at the suffering child, her lips moving silently.

They sat in this vigil for what seemed to Laren half the day, but far less than that, until suddenly Meleden took a great, shaking breath and lay still. Laren rushed her ear to her chest. She heard the little heart beating its rapid rhythm, and then the lungs drew in a shallow breath.

"She seems better," Varial said.

"Yes."

Varial offered to take the child, and Laren carefully shifted her onto the older woman's lap. The leader of the Enre had been coming to her often to instruct her in Askirit ways and beliefs. After Laren had silently stared for a time at the little figures of her friends by the sea, she asked, "If he's the Maker, why does he do this?"

"The sickness?"

"Why make a child like this? Like the blind boy and the maimed girl down by the sea? You keep telling me the Maker loves us. But swords and sickness destroy even children."

"Mysteries," Varial said. "Mysteries around us thick as morning mist. But in the mysteries we find the good. And the greater good that's coming."

They watched the others slowly start their way back up the hill, joined by a group of older children and their teachers. The feeble-minded boy happily traipsed along, always veering off and needing to be pulled back. When they got near, Varial motioned to him. He grinned and came quickly. "Mysteries. Here's one from the Maker. The boy's unaware, yet far happier than you or I." She put a shiny stone in his hand and his grin widened and then he laughed.

Laren took Meleden back into her lap, and the Enre got up to leave. Thinking again about her dream, Laren looked up and asked, "You say you love and follow Auret. But who, truly, is he?"

Varial paused and sat down again. "He is the one sent to us from the Maker. He led our ancestors out of darkness into light. He leads us now to the greater light."

The children chattered around them, then ran off again. Varial was starting to leave again, but Laren added, "Some stories say sierent had no power over him; yet when he descended into Aliare, it battered and crushed him. What powers did he have?"

Varial smiled. "The storms wounded him. But sages say the forces that truly crippled him were from the enemy who loves darkness. The powers used sierent, but Auret used a greater power: the love and faith of a woman—Chaisdyl, who became his mother."

Laren adjusted Meleden on her lap, still wondering about her dream. "Some see Auret as a cripple; others as healed and full of glory. Is he simply what our dreams make of him?"

Varial began reciting long sections of the liturgy to her, telling of Auret's nature. "He is real. But he is also not simply of this world. He is one with the Maker of all worlds, and is at home in all of them."

Laren kept probing but never told Varial about her dream. Finally she forced her eyes up to study the Enre's face as she asked, "You're wise, and you fear no one. You command all the Enre. Why didn't you let them make you queen before Bren came?"

Varial raised her brows. "Because Bren was coming!" She bent over and kissed Meleden. "My life is prayer. Prayer is life. Prayer gives a sense of the times. Perhaps I'll be a queen someday; perhaps an old invalid. The Maker knows. It doesn't matter."

The teachers, dividing the students into several groups for lessons, left as Varial did. Alone with Gresen and the baby, she told her how fearful she had been when Meleden seemed to be dying.

"It would be an enormous loss to us both," Gresen said.

"Perhaps too much loss for me to stand. She's the reason I'm here."

They talked about Askirit beliefs, Ishtel survival, their cultures, men and women. Laren couldn't stifle her suspicion of all men, including Bren.

"He hasn't turned on you yet," Gresen said. "Isn't likely to. Bren has integrity—and he thinks you're the most beautiful woman alive."

"That's what he says."

"Enjoy it!" Gresen's eyes were twinkling behind the wrinkled skin. "He may be right." Then she put her brown hand on Laren's milky face. "I know you don't believe him or us. Among the Askirit, light skin is rare and fine features are rare, so finding you was to Bren like finding a stunning gem. Obviously, most of the rest of us are just an odd mixture of everything." She laughed at herself, her old head dancing. "The Maker made all this marvelous variety—he loves it!" Then her face darkened. "What's evil is how you've felt so ugly. But our people do the same thing. They call Mazcaens 'Snakelips' and 'Maggotmouths.'"

Laren had always heard the opposite description: "Lips like thick, ripe fruit, sensuous and regal." But her own mouth had been an ugly slit in a pointy face.

"It doesn't matter," Laren said.

"It does matter." Gresenpulled Laren's chin up, knowing she didn't like it, but being playful with her. "Laugh a little. If your husband thinks you're beautiful, just laugh a little, learn a little." She winked. "Enjoy his foolishness and our Askirit ignorance."

—— Night Raid ——

The night had been divided into three watches, and for maximum readiness a third of all adults in each village and city came alert for each watch. Bren was getting used to the second watch, the darkest hours, for as he moved from village to village, he wanted to set an example.

The pioneers had preferred caves as they settled the countryside; the original dwellings now faced a variety of new structures made mostly of split rock and stones. The villages were compact, and someone had gotten the idea to stretch across the trails warning strings with balanced pottery.

"Hope some possum doesn't knock over a pot out there," Leas said. He did not think the strings were a very good idea.

"Must happen all the time." Bren sat poised at the very edge of the cave entrance, a sheaf of spears at the ready. Yet his spears seemed weak as sticks. "What are these tales of night terrors? Screeches and chaos. Maybe just our people's fears of the night-world. Or Mazcaens trying to terrify them."

Leas held a keitr launcher and wore a belt bulging with pouches, but he had been pressing Bren about spiritual preparation. "Don't forget the Great Absurdity: that everything depends on our little prayers." His head was shaking for emphasis. "Asel and Yosha and Mela all learned it in the heat of battle. The Absurdity is the one thing necessary."

Bren agreed. "You talk all the time about Mela. Do you sometimes wish you had gone down into the darkness with her?"

The young king had meant it as a nostalgia question, but the usually talkative Leas suddenly fell silent. Bren had almost forgotten his question when Leas finally said, "Yes. Hundreds and hundreds of times I wished I'd gone with her."

"Why didn't you?"

His fingers drummed on his keitr belt. "I've never admitted it to anyone else. I lacked the courage."

Bren patted the handle of the old man's blade. "You seem to have plenty of courage here."

"Maybe." He was rubbing the launcher against his palm. "Mela always thought I'd go with her, you know. And when she came back from down in the pit with that shining face and all that joy, I wept for joy with her. But I wept just as much for me."

Leas dug out his water skin and took a long drink. "Mela had been blind and now saw, and she saw me as I was. But she forgave me. That's what was so remarkable about her. That's why she became queen. All the evil forces of the pit were ranged against her, but she just let the Maker help himself to every piece of her soul."

Leas shook his head, as if he felt foolish.

A rustling sound tensed them. They stroked their weapons, praying out of their fears, a score of their spearmen behind them. Two young blind men nearby grasped keitr pouches and launchers. Bren stiffened at every sound from the night, trying to discern animal noise from attackers.

He felt chilly and damp. Was it his imagination, or was cold, wet air settling on his back? He took several deep breaths; the air coming out of the cave behind him seemed laden with an acrid smell. And with it came something whispering in his mind: "You are food for the night."

"Leas?"

"Don't let them into your mind!"

"What?"

A screech pierced the night, then an agonizing howl. Bren gripped his spears in one hand, his short sword in the other. "What can that be?" He felt the fear in the men at his back and the sense of dark powers converging, howlings and snarlings. A woman screamed; Bren jerked himself upright, wanting to rescue her but not knowing how. His weapons were toys, his boots fastened to the ground. He felt like a worm under a beak.

Worm. Why did that come into his mind? His mind was a jumble of evil whispers: "You are food for worms."

Leas suddenly stood as if rising up out of a lake and said, "We must fling prayers with our spears!" He loudly quoted something from the liturgy.

Bren bolted up beside him. As he prayed aloud with Leas, he felt as if a poison were draining from his body; the howlings and shrieks sounded like men.

The Askirit defenders gripped their spears and rushed into the night toward the village.

The Loft

Laren had arranged for Bren a lunch of dried meat, bread, and apples, knowing he might not show up until evening or even the next day. It was already late afternoon. She picked a little at the bread, wondering if she should go ahead and eat.

He had been gone for nearly a third of a year, and she could not clearly remember just what he looked like. She'd mostly seen him in quick glances, and when he had forced her to look back at him, it made her so uncomfortable her mind fled elsewhere. Now, she kept trying to visualize his face.

Although she had avidly listened to Varial and Gresenwhile Bren was away, she still felt ignorant. The buildings of Belez and Aris were all as alien as distant mountains, and it always felt strange to be inside of one. Her natural habitat was the field and the river's edge and the city dump.

The sound of boots. Were they his boots?

Bren entered the room with a great sigh. "Too long!" He bent to pull off the muddy boots and tossed them into the hall. Turning, he sought her eyes and held out one arm to her, as if to let her choose whether to embrace him or not.

Without hesitating, she crossed the little space between them and put her arms around him.

He hugged her back against his rough clothes with the odors of long travel, pulling her slightly off the floor and burying his face in her neck. He held her tight, saying, "Every night, every night, the pale moon up there, reminding me of you."

She flushed, surprised at how much she loved hearing his words. Regaining her footing she said, "We have some food."

He gave her a squeeze on the shoulder. "How is it—being queen of the Askirit?"

She broke a loaf of bread into portions, eyeing him as he sat down. "Strange. Very strange for an Ishtel."

He arched his brows. "Do people accept you?"

"Everyone but Galial. She'd as soon a donkey were queen."

He laughed with her, accepted a long, crusty piece of bread from her hand, then began briefing her on the war. The kingdom was growing stronger every day. The howlings that had terrified so many had been made by Mazcaens with claws and blades who fled when attacked.

"Do you really have keitr?"

He grinned and held up an apple. "All we have is an ordinary bat about this size. But we also tuck in with him a little reptile, who hates getting launched. When we let fly in the night, he lets out a horrific squeal. Bat wings and reptile's shriek and spears all find their mark at the same time." He bit down on the apple in satisfaction. "They no longer own the terror of the night."

"So now we do?"

He stopped chewing; she dropped her eyes.

Bren pushed back a little from the tray of food and stared at her. "We have to. Otherwise we would all be destroyed."

Her fingers were clicking little polished stones together in an incongruously happy rhythm. "Varial tells me some day the terrors will be over. That's all I meant."

"You've been talking to Varial?" He eased toward her. "Good. The Enre are more spiritual than us all, and they're also the best fighters. Listen well to Varial."

Bren finished eating quickly; she saw him several times glance over at the adjoining room. This time no rushes and scents were laid out, only a loop of big red blossoms on a bed of green moss. Laren walked into the room and picked up the blossoms. "I made this myself."

He lowered his head as she put on him the traditional groom's gift so it hung on his chest. "Who taught you?"

"Gresen, of all people! She's told me the bridal secrets! But—," and here Laren boldly fingered the flowers on his chest, "—she's also told me I should think of you and me as a great joke."

Bren's reaction was what she hoped for—a befuddled collapse of his face. She smiled up at him with playful impudence. "Gresensays men and women have to laugh through all their gropings and fumblings in life." His cheek twitched and his lips pursed; she couldn't tell if he were amused or irritated. "That's the way she said it."

"And what would she know about it?"

Laren clicked the stones in her hand, once again producing the light, happy rhythm. "She was long a wife. She says the Maker is often amused, watching the dance of a woman and a man. And what more unlikely pair could there be than you and I?"

Bren's jaw dipped low in a long grin. He was tired of all this talk and wanted to hold her again. "I'd never thought of the Maker as amused."

"Gresen says he was most serious in making laughter." She put her arms out to him. "But I wouldn't know. I'm just an Ishtel." With exaggerated deliberateness, she looked downward. "Galial thinks our being together is disgusting. I'm trying to see that as funny. It is, don't you think?" She glanced at him, a light smile playing at the corners of her mouth.

He returned her smile. "The celestials would surely agree with you!" He pulled her close again. "Where do you think Gresen got these ideas?"

With a shrewd look Laren said, "From her prayers, perhaps?"

That made Bren smile broadly. "You've been learning Askirit theology. You're smart and beautiful."

As she had seen Askirit do in response to stupid statements, she twisted her nose and snorted out of one nostril. Then she grasped his hand and led him out of the room.

Bren was taken aback by Laren's leading him into the hall. But he followed her to the wide stairway, down two flights, then along a corridor that descended and narrowed until he smelled the smoke and grime of the scullery.

She took his hand again, and he felt like a little boy tagging behind, an odd feeling after commanding an army at war. She was shielding the candle so it threw only a little light, catching occasional highlights of her hair. He was about to protest when she knelt and, with her left hand, quickly counted the wall's decorative slats. She put down the candle, pushed with one hand high and the other low, and a narrow door opened. Thrusting the candle into the opening, she clambered onto a ladder and beckoned him to follow.

Once on the ladder, he could see nothing, but he heard her movements above. He scrambled up, hearing the door close behind. She soon went through an opening, then turned to take his hand and pull him in.

As Laren lighted candles on a table, they revealed a narrow loft with one steeply sloped side. "What is this?"

She eased the little door shut behind them. "Welcome to the king's hiding place. May you never need it to escape your enemies."

At the far end he saw rushes piled high, and on a table, scent strips such as those used by their ancestors in the darkness when they had only touch and sound and smells with which to celebrate a wedding night. "How did you find this place?"

"Varial." Her eyes sparkled with delight at surprising him in his own house. "Varial alone keeps the secret. No one would guess it's here; the ladder goes down to a tunnel to the sea."

He spied a basin that caught rain water from the roof and decided to wash his hands and face. When he was through, she pulled him toward the table. "You don't have to wash up for me." She sniffed. "After all, I'm an Ishtel."

Why did she say that? Was she being a bit sarcastic? No, he decided, she was looking up at him with that impudent smile that made him want to laugh. She took some scents from the table and handed them to him, but she seemed awkward, as if trying to do everything just right. He put the scents in the traditional way into the ringlets of her hair. As he affixed them, he stroked the golden, loose circles, then bent to kiss each one, and then kissed the billows of her soft hair beneath them.

"That's not part of the tradition, is it?" she scolded, her head cocked, but the smile still playing on her lips.

"It's now a new tradition."

Laren kept her eyes off the floor and her fingers busy as she then put the groom scents on Bren. She was smiling, yet he suspected she was mostly repeating her rehearsals, getting every word and movement right, not spontaneously enjoying the moment. Was she genuinely feeling desire for him? "I have no weapons to remove, as is the custom," she was saying. "But I have these." She removed the bindings that held her hair at the sides, then gave her head a quick toss so that it fell fully free.

He pulled her to him and put his fingers deep into her hair, but she ducked away to the biggest heap of rushes and sat back on them, leaning against the wall. She didn't motion for him to come to her but said, "Among your people, the bride is to make preparations . . . and to surprise. I hope I have surprised you." Her eyes flashed down in the Ishtel way, and he wondered why she seemed so awkward, as if giving a little speech. "If a bride is not Askirit, she is to bring a custom of her own people. But the Ishtel have no customs at all."

Laren thrust her arms out in front of her, starting a rhythm with the stones in each hand. "All we have is our songs. And outsiders hear only our sad laments—but there are others. . ." She closed her eyes and started singing with the percussion of the stones in her hand.

Though Bren sat and leaned back beside her, he felt a bit awkward listening and realized he felt that way because Laren was so self-conscious. Her song was a long ballad of love between a young man and woman lost from each other, but finally reunited, then happily running off into the woods together.

After finishing the song, she sat quietly, tapping just two stones together in a steady beat. Then she began a very different kind of song, the words earthy and passionate, full of longing and demand for love. She sang faster and faster, soon jamming her words together and biting them off in fast-clipped phrases. Her head was turned slightly away from him, jerking to the beat, eyes squinted tight. He had heard Ishtels sing passionately about grief and travail, and she now had the same sort of intensity. She snapped the stones together, words tumbling out like water over rapids, singing on and on.

Abruptly she stopped.

He listened to her rapid breathing beside him. "I never heard that kind of Ishtel song before."

She smiled. "Who would have sung it to you?" But then her smile was gone. "It was hard to sing that," she said. "In Belez, men would sing those kind of songs, and I'd bolt away. So I was afraid I'd break down in the middle and ruin it for you." She placed the stones on the rushes. "Actually, it's a lovely song, don't you think?"

He put his face into her hair and sniffed the special scents there. "I never felt you wanted me at all. And I wasn't sure as you sang if your passion was some kind of anger, or if you really wanted me to hold you."

She pushed him playfully. "Want to know which?"

"Yes" He cupped her forearm in his hand and could still feel a little sweat on it. "I want you to feel a little—just a tiny fraction—of what I feel for you."

Laren teased, "There was just a tiny, tiny, tiny desire mixed in there for you. Just the tiniest bit."

They lay on the rushes looking up at a narrow opening showing a thin slice of night sky. The loft seemed to Laren the only truly safe place she had ever found. Like every rabbit and deer, she had always felt vulnerable to predators—Ishtel men who might force her or Mazcaens who might strike her or sacrifice her. Here she felt tranquillity with her lover and protector. The small slice of stars was all the outside reality she wanted let in to her haven.

"Let's stay here forever," she said. "Have food brought. When we want to, we'll escape unseen to the sea. . . ."

He raised himself on his elbow and kneaded her neck. "Sounds good—let Varial take over. I'll just lie here and play with your hair and stare at your beautiful nose."

She wrinkled it at him.

"It's beautiful! Like every part of you." He cupped her face between his palms. "You're more lovely than those stars. And if you still deny that, you're oblivious."

Chapter 7.

—— That Great, Dark City ——

Bren was wedged in a chimney formation on the peak above Belez. Sweaty from hauling his share of the wood, he had climbed up here to let the wind blow on his face and to look down on his prey.

All was ready for the assault on the city.

"Grab 'im!"

The sharp cry from behind thrust into Bren like a shard of ice. He turned and rushed down from his perch, nostrils flaring to confront the fool who had cried out. Clambering over a boulder shaped like a fat gourd, he dropped on its other side and spied two soldiers wrestling with a near-naked, scrawny Ishtel. They had him pinned under their knees, like a squirming white worm under two crows.

"What's the matter with you men!"

One soldier's head jerked a little toward him, but they kept wrestling the man down. They were hog-tying his ankles and wrists together behind him, but he kept kicking and biting. Without looking up one soldier said, "He tried to fling himself off! If I hadn't yelled, his wretched little body would have smashed itself right at Belez's front door."

He got a loop over an ankle and a wrist, snugged it tight, and then looked up. When he saw it was the king standing above him, his face went pale. He mumbled thickly, "The Ishtel stays quiet, then suddenly tries to bolt over the edge."

Teeth ground tight, Bren bent over to look at the man. Even with his jaw pressed flat on the rocks, his blinking eyes looked down, his face twitching in terror.

"Fasten the ropes on his wrists, but loosen his feet. Stand him up."

The soldiers yanked him to his feet, furious at him that he had gotten them into trouble.

"Easy," Bren said. He had them drape a jacket on him and bring him to the fire. It was cold up on the peak, and he watched as the soldiers tried to get a hot drink past his shaking lips. They sat him on a rock; he kept shivering, looking like a skinned squirrel with a baggy jacket hanging on him.

"Why kill yourself?" Bren demanded. "We won't hurt you."

The Ishtel's eyes flashed across Bren's face in a bitter glance of disbelief, then bore into the ground. "I'd rather splat on the rocks than be burned on the peak."

Bren looked around at the many stacks of wood set to ignite. "You're not here to be sacrificed!"

The Ishtel's eyes stayed down, and he took a great, shuddering breath. His hand reached out for the bread placed beside him, and he angled his mouth as he opened it to get it between his five teeth, all on one side of his narrow jaw.

"We attack the city tonight," Bren said. "You were brought here only to answer questions."

The man chewed and gummed the bread, still shivering. "Questions. Questions. Ishtels don't know anything." He gave a mournful downward sweep of his head, like a beaten, ingratiating mongrel.

"My wife is an Ishtel."

The captive gave no sign that he thought this remarkable. With his jaw set at a preposterous angle, he used his five teeth to rip off another piece of bread and then gulped it down.

"My wife was terrified up here, like you are. But we were on this peak a long time. Night or day, nothing strange happened."

The Ishtel chewed noisily without answering.

"Her name is Laren. Did you know her? Now she's free, and she's queen of all the Askirit."

The man bolted upright, head lowered, eyes on his feet, but his voice coming out with surging force. "Of course I know your queen is an Ishtel! Does Belez talk of anything else?" His obsequious mannerisms were belied by the rage in his voice; he stared down as if he would burn holes into the rocks.

Bren sympathized with his anger and said, "It's criminal you have to live in rags, eating garbage and cowering like animals." He couldn't resist reaching under the man's chin and forcing his head up so that he could look at him. The face that glared back was full of hatred.

"I only want to help you. I want to help the Ishtels. Laren the queen is—"

"Don't I know it! Don't I know it!" The man's eyes were blazing. Bren's hand jerked away and fell to his side. "No one hated us Ishtels before you came. Not like they hate us now." He spat on the rocks. "An Ishtel a queen? Sacrilege! An Ishtel, of all things, up on the sacred peak? Desecration! Don't I know your queen's an Ishtel! You've got them hating us more than they hate you."

Bren cleared his throat to say something, but the Ishtel flopped his hand to the jacket collar and shoved the cloth down, displaying deep burns on his throat and angling down his chest. "Every time they lose a battle, it's the Ishtels' fault." He yanked the collar back up. "Half the Ishtels in Belez are dead, and the other half wish they were."

The man took a gigantic gulp of air. During the rush of words, his eyes had been at his feet. Now they flashed past Bren's face and fell once again to the ground.

Bren sat a long time, eyes down like those of the Ishtel beside him chewing noisily.

Leas clambered up beside him, breaking into his mood. Ridged with keitr belts, he grinned at Bren with enormous satisfaction. His blind young men, after a recent quake, had actually discovered keitr—and the old teacher could barely contain himself. "Thirty men, each with two full belts. For them, blind all their lives, it will be just like the old wars in the darkness."

Bren remembered going to the place where the students had found keitr. The quake had left a wide rift, and by the time he had arrived, Leas had already been down into the cave and confirmed they were indeed keitr. "Hanging there upside-down, just like our stone models!"

"How do you know they're not just a different kind of bat?"

Offended, Leas had made a loud popping sound with his fists. "Keitr are not bats!" Then he had said soberly, "Look down into the rift. The young men have already started the gathering. It's very dangerous. We'll likely have deadly proof."

Laren had come with Bren, insisting, because she knew many of the students. "How can you let these boys go down there?" she demanded.

Leas was busily adjusting an inner sleeve for a pouch. "Scratches mean only some fever and scars; it's the bite that kills." He was already pulling on the thick protective skins.

"They're only boys."

"No! Young men. All of them older than initiation age." A thick leather hood now covered his head; his eyes glared out at her passionately, like a ferret from a hole. "All their lives they've practiced gathering. They know the danger. They want to feel live keitr in their hands being rammed into pouches. They want to launch them against Mazcaens."

They gathered the live keitr, but one young man, too close when something spooked the cave, was bitten and later died. Now, waiting to attack Belez, Bren kept seeing Laren's face as, with old Askirit rites, they had buried the boy in the sea. She seemed to feel more agony than them all, as if he were her closest kin.

They were blind, he thought. She was Ishtel.

"We found the keitr just in time," Leas was saying. "The Mazcaens were figuring out we didn't really have them."

Bren nodded. The young men had belts bulging with live keitr, anxious to begin the assault. Yet he was apprehensive. He knew Belez and its weaponry and fortifications. It had been Varial's comment that had set him resolutely toward the enemy capital: "We can't be at war forever with the Mazcaens. They hate us now more than ever. Someday their stronghold will have to be rooted out." To Bren, when the keitr were found, it had been a sign. But he asked Leas, "Do you think we'll find some peace when this is done?"

"I pray so," Leas said. "But only the Maker knows if we'll have peace—or even a world to have it in."

Sacred Fire

Behind the great city, Varial was describing to Bren how the Enre would scale the massive formations rising behind it. Skilled with piton and steely fingers, the women would silently take out the small contingent of guards. The Mazcaens would not dream the Askirit would strike in force up these sheer cliffs, which was why Bren had most of his troops massed here.

Varial figured the Enre were more than halfway up. Bren was trying to distinguish in the darkness the top of the soaring formations when a patch of sky began to glow pink. It defined the top of the cliffs in a long, ragged line, and he strained to see if he could spot figures moving on it. The glow grew brighter and became red, like the beginning of a midnight dawn, glowing eerily in the starless sky.

The fires had been lighted just before the Enre were due to capture the heights. All Belez would be staring at the fiery, sacred peak.

They listened and watched, hearing nothing and seeing nothing but the red glow. Bren wondered what the Mazcaens were thinking as the peak that dominated every thought had suddenly come alive in the night.

Ropes tumbled down the walls, and Varial gave the signal. Bren led the squads of spearmen and men with keitr as they ran to grab the dangling ends.

Step after step, grip after grip on the ropes, they moved like a legion of beetles up the wall. Halfway up, Bren felt terribly vulnerable and thought it was taking too long. If the alarm were sounded, the enemy could cut the ropes or rain rocks down on them. But the ropes held steady, and soon Bren was on the top, walking among masses of troops. Silently adjusting spears and blades, they were bunched in a thick line along the city's rear perimeter.

At Bren's signal, the squads stalked forward, the only light the red glow in the sky. With so many men moving, it was hard to follow the narrow trails this far back from the temple. The Enre had gone ahead to silence anyone between them and the city, but Bren worried he would hear a shout any instant.

But then they were in front of the temple and the murals. Bren knew that a mere spear's throw in front of them, thousands of defenders would be massed at the city's wall. The red glow in the sky had become dimmer but was still bright enough to reveal the top of the wall and the edges of buildings.

The plan called for the enemy to be staring up at the lighted peak, backs to the temple, unprepared for what was to come. At Bren's signal, hundreds of men stood, stepped forward, grasped their atlatals, and then launched sheaves of spears high into the air at the Mazcaen positions. Then scores of keitr were launched.

As the spears were airborne, there was a strange moment of silence, as if the little army itself were suspended in an unreal drama. Then the spears struck, and the resultant roar jarred them as they reloaded their atlatals. Keitr screamed and bit, injecting their poison. Shouts and harsh Mazcaen commands seemed right in Bren's face as he signaled to release another volley, then another and another.

Spears and keitr gone, they grasped their swords and charged directly at the gate, shouting ferociously to break them at their center and send them fleeing. Bren was counting on the effect of the spears and keitr and the flaming peak and the din of the charging enemy in the darkness to shatter their will. His own voice was strained by his shouts as he saw the dark form of an enemy right in front of him and thrust his sword at it.

His sword struck something hard and clanged, wrenching his wrist painfully. A roar of rage came at him from the man, and Bren was stunned to hear that roar coming from a thousand throats in front of him. The ferocious shouts of his own troops were being drowned out by overwhelming screams of fury, as if every enemy soldier's throat had become a quake splitting the air and reverberating at them like a tidal wave. Enemy bodies intent on annihilating them surged forward and Bren felt a shoulder strike his chest at the same instant a blade pierced his belly. He crumpled as the tide of momentum reversed and enemy soldiers trampled over him.

Bren's legs spasmed even as a boot crashed into his pelvis, and then another hit square on his face, the heel glancing off and grinding into his shoulder. The pain from his wound radiated upward, dimming everything else as enemy troops stormed past him.

He found himself floating above the melee, looking down on it and thinking that he had done exactly the wrong thing. The fires on the peak had infuriated the enemy soldiers when they realized they were set by the Askirit—the same enemies who had defiled it before. All their terror had turned to rage. Bren looked down at his troops being overrun and slaughtered. If only I hadn't lighted the fires, he thought, if only we had just melted over the walls and attacked in the darkness.

Then the scene was gone, and he was walking along a gushing torrent of water. On the other side was the figure of a woman, and she was beckoning to him.

Somehow he knew it was Mela, the queen. She motioned him to leap over the torrent, but he wanted to make right what was happening below him. All his plans and desires for the kingdom, for the Ishtels. . . . He looked down but saw only thick, green grass under his feet.

Mela pointed downstream, to a little bridge, and he walked slowly to it. He put a foot on it, then the other, feeling the peace like warm fog floating toward him and enveloping him. In an instant he was on the other side, and Mela wrapped her arms around him.

He felt the need to kneel before her, but she knew his thoughts and laughed. "You are a king yourself!"

"No longer."

"Yes!" she exclaimed with irrepressible merriment. "Auret has made us all royal here."

"But how can I stay? The battle!" He did not want to go back, though he felt he had betrayed everyone. "Laren. Gresen. The child."

Mela motioned him toward a wide field thick with flowers. "Bren, all is well. Don't you think they too will fulfill all the Maker's thoughts?"

News from the Front

A woman had rushed into Laren's room moments before. "Varial is coming!" Her one hand had pointed down the hall, the other nervously fingering her hair. Then she had disappeared.

Laren had heard rumors of disaster. Now truth was walking down the hallway toward her, and she had no desire to meet it.

Varial quick-stepped into the room, disheveled, a bold bruise standing out red and angry on her forehead. Her eyes sought out

Laren's and the instant they connected made her certain the rumors had been right.

The Enre leader held out her palms in condolence. "Bren is dead." Laren had expected that. Why, then, the tears suddenly coming so heavily they turned Varial's face into a watery image. She turned away and wiped her eyes.

"You came to love Bren, didn't you?" Varial slowly eased herself into a chair, as if she had many more bruises under her clothing. "Bren was worth loving." She put her head back and closed her eyes. "But at Belez, the hope he brought was crushed. Now the air is full of doom, as if Bren had never come."

Laren swallowed and blinked away more tears. "Now I'll lose Meleden too, and you, and everything I love." In contrast to Varial, who was sinking yet deeper into the chair, Laren was taking short, brisk steps from window to table to bench, eyes peering down the hallway, out the window, and then back to study Varial's face. "And Leas?" she asked. "And the blind boys?"

"All dead, as far as we know."

Laren looked away and felt her knees weaken. She gripped a window ledge. "What is required of me now?"

Varial lifted one heavy eyelid. "You are the queen."

Laren gave a little snort. "Bren's little oddity. His golden-haired pet."

She expected Varial to object, but she said nothing, eyes closed, breathing slowly as if drawing her body and soul together.

"I'm the queen, but all I've done is hold babies and learn Askirit ways."

A little smile played on the corners of Varial's mouth. "But you're an Ishtel." The smile widened beneath her closed eyes, as if she were savoring the irony. "An Ishtel learns to survive, like a bristle pine against coastal winds." She opened her eyes and looked at Laren like an old owl. "And the Ishtel I know is smart. Smart enough to survive."

Laren looked out the window at a woman in the street walking with two small children. "In Belez I always felt such shame at being an Ishtel. Except once. It was after my mother was dead."

She watched the three figures amble slowly down the road, the children moving from one object to another, as if the city existed for them to explore. "Even in the garbage dumps I didn't belong. After all, it wasn't our garbage."

Varial was sunk deep in the chair, her half-opened eyes studying her.

"The forest wasn't mine, either, but I pretended it was, always worried about hairy things behind the trees that would want a little girl for their dinner. And looking out for the wild Ishtel."

Varial's eyes crinkled. Laren raised her brows. "You think all Ishtels are wild? No! But everyone talked about this Ishtel who said no words but made horrible squawks and was as damp and buggy as the swamps he lived in."

Laren opened wide her mouth and snapped her teeth with exaggerated ferocity. "And he bit the heads off squirrels." She grinned. "That's what they told me, so I was always terrified I'd see him. Yet I couldn't stay away from the woods, and one day, there he was, right in front of me, sitting on a big tree branch, hair flung out wispy and tangled and long as his beard. His bright eyes bored into me, but after an instant of fright, I realized he was scared. He was just an old, broken Ishtel."

"What did he say?"

"He couldn't speak, but he motioned me closer. He spelled out his meanings with sighs and tremblings, never saying what was wrong with him but making signs that he'd once had children. He wept as his hands made shapes for two boys and a girl. From then on, I looked for him in the woods every day. His face would light up when he'd see me, and for that instant it was okay to be me."

Varial sat up a little. "Even good to be you?"

Laren nodded. "Yes, even good. He was Ishtel, I was Ishtel, and for that instant—when his face would light up at seeing me—it was good to be Ishtel." She threw up her hands in amazement, as if she had just made an absurd statement. She tipped her head and let a long shock of her golden hair fall into her palm, then let it slide away. "Once I went looking, and he was gone. I never stopped searching, never stopped thinking of the way he'd look at me—his old broken face lighted up as if I was all in the world he loved."

"Ever feel that way again?"

"Only when I had the dream about Auret."

Varial was no longer slouched and gimlet-eyed. She was sitting upright, ears cocked for every word. "All my life I've felt that way about Auret."

Galial stepped into the room with Meleden, filling the doorway with her bulk. Laren went to take the child. "And I felt that way when I first held Meleden; it was like a familiar echo."

"We've each felt that," Galial said, trying to enter the conversation, obviously not wanting to leave the room.

"That's why we took such a risk to bring you with us," Laren said pointedly.

"Good thing." Galial looked defensive and desperate for information, but not about to admit any debt.

Laren hoisted Meleden onto her chest so that her head rested on her shoulder. "She somehow brings peace with her."

With a flicking of her fingers, Varial motioned that Galial should leave. "We need to talk about what you face as queen."

Laren shook her head. "Let her stay. She knows all my weaknesses, and she can tell me all the reasons an Ishtel should never rule."

Varial angrily wrinkled her face. "And what are those, Galial?"

The freed slave looked sullenly downward and did not reply.

"You're the only one who can rule!" Varial pronounced firmly.

Laren eased the baby to her side and sat down. "Varial, they'd make you queen right now. They want someone to lead, and that's you."

The Enre warrior had roused herself from the chair, and now she set her jaw in a rigid line. "Yes, I love command. I was made for it. And that's just why I cannot—will not—be queen."

Laren studied Varial's clenched jaw and tight eyes. She seemed to be forcing herself to state every word: "My pride must be ground fine by the Maker. No, you, Laren, will remain queen—and regent."

Galial muttered, "You brought this on by stealing the child."
Laren stared at her in disbelief. "Rescued, you mean!"

Galial nodded, but it was clear she had needed to say something in protest.

"You are needed to establish the kingdom," Varial said, looking with disgust at Galial. "But I will lead your armies."

A warning flashed through Laren. Was Varial manipulating her, using her somehow?

"The Askirit take great pride in their golden Ishtel," Varial was saying. "You're magical and foreign and clever—and linked to Bren's hope, which they're desperate to regain."

"What choices do I have?"

Varial didn't reply. Laren bit her lip and thought about a wild old Ishtel's white hair and beard ruffling in the wind.

—— Proclamations ——

Laren stood at the foot of the great aisle of the King's House, feeling thousands of eyes on her. She wore the thorns of mourning, unseen beneath the thin vines of purple leaves and magenta flowers cascading from the crown of her head down the full length of her hair. The leaves and blossoms celebrated death as entry into light, but the thorns the grief of those left behind.

Varial reached over, as if to adjust Laren's hair, but in brushing the thorns back from her forehead purposely made several long scratches in her skin. It made Laren furious to feel the sting and then the thin lines of blood forming. The day before, Varial had insisted she scratch herself and let a little blood drip, as was the custom. Laren had flatly refused.

Now she wondered what other impertinence might come from the one who could have been queen but insisted the honor and duties be hers. "Many are grumbling," Varial had admitted. "They resent the idea of a foreigner ruling over them." Now, by Varial's cool demeanor, Laren knew she was nervous, anxious that nothing go wrong.

Laren started forward at the head of the procession, stepping into the bright shaft of light streaming down on the center aisle. She felt like a spectacle as people craned their necks and many stood to watch her pass. She was unaware of how the light played on her golden hair, with leaves and blossoms highlighting it, unaware of how the little ridges of blood and the trickle over her cheekbone gave her a courageous look. When she mounted the dais at the brightest confluence of light, she had no thoughts about her appearance at all. But she was acutely aware of the people's desperation.

Their fear was more pronounced than when Bren had stood not long ago in this same place. Their king and only hope had been killed, his army devastated. Raids had already resumed, only this time with the fury from an enemy whose holy ground had been desecrated. Thousands of Mazcaen troops were said to be massed outside Aris.

Laren felt their panic, and she had decided she had nothing to lose in asserting herself. It was her skin at risk, for the Mazcaens hated her. The effrontery of her now becoming regent would inflame them even more.

The officials were barely done making pronouncements and adding Bren's pectoral around her neck when she stepped in front of Varial. The Enre was supposed to address them about battle plans and to rouse them to hope before Laren pronounced her benediction. But, still angry about the thorns, she said to all the people with conviction, "We must make Aris impenetrable! Every man, every woman, every child a warrior." She held high a blade and moved it under the light as Bren had done. She spoke of aggressive patrols and driving out the enemy and that they would complete what Bren had started.

Though she spoke loudly, her voice barely carried in the great hall. Yet it made everyone strain to hear her, which made them all the more attentive. Most had never heard her voice before, and none thought her capable of such convictions and determination. When she finished, they wildly applauded her.

Laren then told them Varial would command the military. The Askirit woman stepped beside her and affirmed her words, adding many of her own, and then stepped back for the queen to lead the recessional.

After the ceremonies, Laren went directly to the strategy room where she had asked to meet with Varial alone. When the door was closed behind them, the Enre leader said, "You changed our agreement."

Laren whirled around to face her. "So did you. I wore the leaves and the thorns, but I told you I wouldn't cut my skin."

Varial huffed. "I broke no agreement. I gave you an appropriate scratch, the custom for every Askirit who mourns."

"You went against the queen's wishes!" Laren forced herself to stare intently at the forceful woman.

Varial eyed her carefully. "You had not yet become regent. I wanted to make sure you did. My loyalty is to Auret and to the nation."

Laren never dropped her gaze, holding it steady for a long, long time until Varial finally added, "And to you."

"I may be an Ishtel, but I won't be a puppet. I'm smart enough to know a queen like that won't survive." Her words were strong, but she found she was looking at the ground in the Ishtel way.

"Your words were inspiring." Varial was pulling up her chin the way Bren used to. "You said it just as I would have, and I've already given the orders. But the truth is, we're much worse off than we admitted."

Laren ignored her having raised her chin. "That's what I sense. And you and I will be special delicacies on the spits of Belez. It's all I've been thinking about."

"Your thinking once produced the plan to rescue Meleden in a bucket."

The new queen grunted. "We may have to do something even more improbable. Like going back into Belez."

Varial grimaced and vigorously shook her head. "Did you see me when I returned from there?"

"Did you see me when the bucket slipped in front of the guards?"

They sat in silence for a very long time. Varial had pulled her blade from its sheath and kept rapping her knuckles against it. Finally Laren said, "They'd never expect it. All their resources are poised to attack Aris."

"That's why we need every soldier here."

"With every man, woman, and child armed, half can defend the city. The other half can help take Belez."

Varial snapped knuckle against palm. "Help? Help who?"

Laren purposely kept her eyes on the floor. "Ishtels. And the new Ishtel queen."

Chapter 8.

──── Swamps ────

A wet branch snapped across Laren's temple when she stretched from log to hummock in the swamp outside Belez. *Am I being reckless coming here?* she wondered. Galial couldn't keep her exasperation to herself; every time she snapped a branch or stumbled, she hissed. At times Laren regretted she had brought her, yet Galial knew the tunnels under Belez, knew the vital little secrets.

With three Enre they had slipped through the enemy forests and circled far around the city to the long, narrow swamp with buttes on either side. Laren wiped a bug from her face and got mud on her cheek. Her mouth twisted in a wry smile, thinking, *Here we are, five women skulking through the swamp to topple a kingdom.*

They emerged on stony clay and scrub pine, wary that someone had heard them thrashing over the tangled brush. One of the superbly trained Enre scouted forward, then returned to take the point as the other Enre flanked Laren and Galial.

Laren knew if the Ishtels saw her first, they might try to kill her, knowing she had brought all this persecution on them. Yet she also knew where the Ishtels had gone when they had been driven out of Belez. The place fugitive Ishtels always fled, past the swamps and through its narrow gorge to the hard-scrabble woods no one but Ishtels would visit.

All five carried huge packs; the Enre on the point signaled, dropped to her knees, and opened her pack. "Dried meat and fruit," she called out. "Corn. Come and eat!"

She repeated it loudly three times before a man in rags emerged, took the small packet from her, and fled back into the woods. Others came after him, men and women and children, accepting one packet each, then backing away. The two other Enre joined her and handed out their food. The Ishtels gulped it down, glancing repeatedly at the strange women kneeling in the barren woods.

When Laren and Galial joined them, Ishtel heads jerked up. Though Laren wore simple leggings and jacket, they had never seen an Ishtel clothed so well, nor with such a bold look. They were non-plused, eyes glancing over her, fingers stuffing food into their mouths, feet set to run.

Laren knelt and opened her pack. "Come and eat," she said, palms open toward her pack and Galial's.

Would her people try to kill her?

No one moved as the Ishtels studied her with their quick glances. Finally some children came, and as they received their little packets of food, adults started rushing forward, eyes darting to her face. The food was quickly gone, with hundreds of Ishtels taking their distance, licking crumbs from the corners of their mouths. More joined them on the fringes, latecomers who would get no food. Laren had thought long about what she would say at this moment.

She stood and loudly declared, "We could carry just so much food!" She spoke not apologetically, like an Ishtel, but like a ruler. "Do you want to fill your bellies? Fill them day after day?" She held up her empty pack. "Why can't you? Why are Ishtels always hungry—always, always hungry? And why are Mazcaens stuffed like sows?" She let the silence hang between them, then said bitingly, "Because the Mazcaens have always taken the food for themselves. They chew up the fat ears of corn and leave you cobs. They roast and eat great slabs of meat and leave you gnawed, rancid bones."

Laren surveyed the faces in front of her and saw several old men with long white hair and beards. She thought of the old man of the woods, and her voice nearly sputtered with anger: "Who said Ishtels should starve? That they are useless? Some Mazcaen tale-spinners in the darkness below? Mazcaens who came into the light still hating us?"

Her fist was up in the air; she looked up at it as if it had simply appeared there. She opened its palm out to the dejected Ishtels in rags. "You all know I've become queen of the Askirit. An outrage. A crime against the natural order. Hah!" She watched for reactions but saw none. "An outrage? But I've learned Ishtels are clever. I've learned the Maker considers us more valuable than gems. Think of that!"

Laren studied them, her mouth lifted in the slightest suggestion of a smile as she thought of telling them they were beautiful. Not only would they think that absurd, they wouldn't care. All they thought about was food, and she knew she must emphasize that again and again. "Look at how I have been fed. We will feed you too. Feed you all you want, bring you this very night into the granaries of Belez. Why should you fear what they can do to you?" She described in great detail how they would eat till they were full, and then she said, "But first you have to help us overthrow the Mazcaens. This is your one chance. They despise all of us, and they want us to stay hungry forever."

The Ishtels moved like wraiths through the dead of night, driven through the swamps and then the city by their hunger and promises of raiding the granaries before dawn. All their lives they had tried not to be seen, and now with relatively few soldiers left in the city, hundreds were soon padding stealthily in the corridors under the royal buildings.

Laren passed the doorway where she had lugged the water bucket with Meleden past the guards. The corridor was deserted, only one lone candle burning.

She bounded up the half flight of stairs to the storage level, Ishtels padding behind her. She passed the clothing bins where the red-haired princess had humiliated her, then turned and climbed the long flight up, pulse racing that she should be penetrating the royal residence. She had always viewed these rooms like the sacred peak; to enter them now made her flush with shame and exhilaration.

The guards were completely unprepared. Like a cloud of ragged moths, the Ishtels overwhelmed them so softly she wondered if the royal families were even awakened. But as she cautiously entered the widest, most ornate doorway, the king stood in a brocade gown with a candle in one hand, a jeweled sword in the other.

Laren stepped back, closer to the score of Ishtels behind her. "We will not harm you. Put down your sword."

The man glared. Laren took one step closer and watched the candlelight play over his coarse, apoplectic face. He grimaced at the sudden sound of gates crashing open outside, and then sounds of alarm.

"Too late," Laren said. "The gates are down and Askirit troops and Enre are storming the city. They'll find little resistance, for the sentries have all been silenced."

She forced herself to hold his gaze, staring into those regal eyes, until at last he dropped them. Then he looked up again, tensed for a second and then bellowed. Laren reached for her blade, thinking he would charge her with his sword and that the Ishtels would run from the king's wrath. But he stood stock still, howling, muscles around his eyes twitching and his jaw grinding, as if he wanted all of them between his teeth.

Laren took one step closer. "Do you know who did all this?" she asked. "Ishtels. The Ishtels you drove out of Belez. Ishtels like me. Snake-bellied, flat-lipped, garbage-eating Ishtels."

The Queen's Mercy

The third day after the fall of Belez, Laren at last believed their victory would not be reversed by a counterattack. They had positioned their troops and sent Enre back to Aris with news and orders. Laren had put Galial in charge of the slaves, who were quick to please, though told they were now free. Best of all, many hundreds of Ishtel men had joined the ranks. Each Askirit soldier had two Ishtels to train and to fight beside. They could therefore send half their strike force back to Aris, yet still defend the city.

The Ishtels stood among the Askirit veterans, dressed in scrounged uniforms and looking sloppy and unpredictable. At Varial's urging, Laren now stood before them on the reviewing stand of the defeated king, who stood nearby roped to other prisoners. "You Ishtels have freely chosen to fight beside us," she said in as loud a voice as she could muster. "Learn from the Askirit beside you. And, Askirit soldiers, do not despise the Ishtels. Their eyes dart to the ground, but as Varial says, they are clever in ways you will not expect. Learn from them, as they learn from you."

She nodded toward the prisoners. "We would not have taken the city from them without the Ishtels. Today, we are all Askirit. We all seek the light and the Maker. And we are all Ishtels, for your queen is Ishtel."

The soldiers returning to Aris marched in high spirits out of the city while in the opposite direction the roped king, priests and officials were led toward the temple. They looked remarkably like the prisoners Laren had often seen led through the city in a long line.

The temple was the largest building of all, the center of the great complex at the center of Belez. Varial and Laren climbed the steep, wide stairs, the line of prisoners and guards trailing incongruously behind them like a dark tail. At the top they were stopped by a massive wall soaring to the top of the building, broken only by ten small, dark doorways cramped in a low line at the bottom.

Varial stooped to enter one. "Soldiers have explored all this. Come on."

Laren envied the Enre who had no fears of this place. For her, it was far different. To have been raised in Belez was to sense the temple always dominating the city, this heart of terror always beating for her and for everyone who might displease the powers. She could barely force her feet to enter the opening and begin descending the steep stairs with walls close on either side crowding at her.

Though plenty of candles were lighted, the corridor's irregularity and sudden rooms, which appeared like swellings in a snake, cast shadows that made Laren desperate to emerge into larger space. They kept descending; she thought they must be deep underground when they finally stepped out on a level floor. A few steps and they emerged into daylight in a large oval space. Ten small, low doorways ringed it, and an oval altar was raised waist high at its center.

Laren looked up at the oval walls narrowing at the top, the oval of light streaming down the same size as the altar it struck. She looked back at the altar, feeling dizzy from the sloping perspective. She said quietly to Varial, "They had only the night coming down on them when they sacrificed." She then noticed the priest, hands trussed behind his back, staring at her.

She fought the hatred welling up toward this man who had officiated at so many ceremonies.

"So you will kill us on the altar," he hissed. "But you'll feel its curse. You can't desecrate it and live."

"How so?" Varial asked evenly.

The man's eyes were locked on Laren's hair. "Not even a bone of an Ishtel can touch the altar."

Despite her new power, Laren felt his sneer hit her like a blow. She walked over and deliberately put a hand on the altar. "We Ishtels are not even worthy to die." She looked for the first time at its center; an oval hole dropping down into darkness.

Varial, repulsed but fascinated by the pagan rites, said to the prisoners, "You have been brought here to explain the sacrifices."

The king lifted his head defiantly. "Sacrifices are necessary. All would die if a few did not."

Varial spun toward him. "But you never sacrificed your own!"

The king shook his head wearily. "Don't you realize how dependent we all are on the gods?"

"But on the altar you desecrate what is holy: innocent children. How many of their bones lie beneath us?"

The king did not answer, nor did the priests, though Varial stared at them one by one.

Laren deeply regretted giving in to Varial's insistence she come here. She hated this talk and this place. Her eyes kept returning to the oval of light far above. What did she know of all the religion and evil done here, and what did she care? Varial, so deeply religious herself, was asking the Mazcaens if fiends from the pit whispered in their ears, but Laren had no desire to hear more. She gripped a captain's shoulder and pointed to the doorway; without saying a word she slipped away from the voices and the altar, climbing that long, long way back up to the light.

In the outside air, she kept walking, down to the river where she had so often washed clothing and stared at the great peak with both dread and awe. What did she know about this? All that was clear to her was the peace that flowed from Meleden and the certitude and love from Bren and the sense the Maker loved her, none of which she had felt in the depths of that temple.

"I felt it too." Laren turned toward the captain who had spoken. "The oppression down there. I don't see how you could have lived in this city."

Laren summoned the royal child who had once slapped her. The girl arrived at the river wearing bright new clothing and a sullen, imperious look.

"I told them to let you choose your own clothes instead of prisoner's garb. We do not make war on children."

"I am not a child."

She was perhaps thirteen; her name was Sanith. Laren had often thought of taking sweet revenge on her, but then she would force herself to think of Meleden. She wanted that peace, and she sensed it did not come through revenge.

Six soldiers flanked the girl, two of them Ishtels. Sanith had pointedly moved away from them.

"Do you remember when you struck me across the face?"

The girl's eyes accosted Laren's like weapons. "I should have killed you. Every day I think I should have killed you."

Laren forced herself to laugh, but the sound emerged high and hollow. "If you had me now, as I have you," she said, leaning back, "you would roast me over a slow fire. And enjoy every moment of it."

"You would deserve every moment of it!" Sanith's lips were pursed in tight certainty. This Ishtel traitor had violated all natural order, had ruined the world with her sacrilege.

"And what do you deserve, since you struck the queen of the Askirit?"

"Queen?" Her lips curled in disgust. "I deserve honor, for I am the king's niece!"

All her years, the girl had known only the upper rooms of the palace; Laren despaired of reaching her. "The Maker has made us all to love each other. He made us all—that is what I've learned in Aris. And you should be very glad I have come to believe it."

She took Sanith with her to inspect the palace, where she had asked Galial to meet her. When they arrived at the vast wardrobe room, she was already there supervising. Several Ishtel children were trying on the royal clothing; the outfits hung from them like sacks on sticks.

The children were overwhelmed with disbelief and delight. Laren laughed as they wriggled into one outfit after another and danced and swirled.

Suddenly Galial recognized the royal child standing beside the guards. She stopped in mid-motion as if she had once again been slapped across the face. Slowly she turned, studying the girl's sour face staring in rage at this desecration of her most holy place, the wardrobe room.

Galial walked over to Sanith, grasped her hair in her fingers like the top of a sack and with one hand lifted her by it so she dangled in the air in front of her. Then she put her big, wide face against the girl's small, narrow one, nearly smashing it. "You cannot imagine how fortunate you are, child, that the queen has spoken for you." Galial lowered her just a little, dangling her by her hair, the girl's face a wincing mass of tightened muscles. When she finally screamed, Galial laughed at her and dropped her to the floor. "I didn't scream when you struck me." She then turned back to the Ishtel children.

Laren watched the score of former slaves and Ishtels staring, the world once again turned upside down before them, the little girl now struggling to stand but letting a tear roll down her cheek without wiping it.

The queen left the room, taking Sanith with her as she continued to inspect the city, hoping the royal child's mind would open just a crack. At the place Laren had spent much of her life foraging for food—the garbage pits—she said to her, "Suppose you were born an Ishtel, and every day you dug here desperate for something to eat. Suppose you were born in a field to people with nothing."

The girl's expression stayed stoic. "But I wasn't, was I?" Sanith wrinkled her nose at the stench. "But you were." And she said this last as if that had been a very proper thing.

At dawn next morning, Laren was again at the river, this time alone, watching waves swirl over boulders. She had little hope her compassion would mean anything to the red-haired child. She had felt such revulsion and weakness in her descent into the depths of the temple that it had kept her wakeful much of the night.

The only thing that lightened her heart was remembering how Bren had talked about the celestials, that even in devastation, they saw everything from the heights. They could be lighthearted and full of mirth despite horrors and evil. She set her mind on that, kept coming back to it and all the teachings about the light from the liturgy and the sages.

Varial stepped past the guards nearby and sat beside her. "You disappeared on me yesterday."

Laren kept her eyes on the roiling currents. "I told you I never wanted to go down there."

The Enre sighed. "The queen cannot flinch from her duties."

She decided not to comment on that. Instead Laren asked, "Did you execute the men down there?"

"Of course not. The queen must decide that."

"With much help from her counselors." Laren wrapped the stem of a purple flower around her small finger, making a ring of it. "Let's not spar." She smiled, her eyes crinkling. "Remember how Bren said the celestials joked about stuffing him back into his body. He kept saying they could find humor in anything. And since you have said I am clever, I have been looking very industriously for the humor in Belez."

She called for the king to be brought to them. When he arrived, she had him sit on the grass near the water. The tall, muscular guards near him looked like trees beside a hunched animal.

"I have very bad news for you," she announced. The king looked up at her but said nothing. "All these years, you've had the symbols of the city all wrong. The torn pennants, the great figures of the kings, they're all wrong."

She watched for a reaction, but he simply glared. She leaned toward him and whispered dramatically, "We've learned that Mazc himself was an Ishtel!" She leaned back into the grass, twisting the flower ring on her finger.

He shared none of the mirth on Laren's face.

"Mazc the legend, an Ishtel!" she declared. "How do I know? An Ishtel told me." She grinned. "How do you know Mazc was Mazcaen? A Mazcaen told you!" She was deliberately goading him, not for anyone's sake but her own, to attack what had tormented her all her life, to attack in a way that did not give in to the blood lust tempting her to revenge.

"You made up myths—so can we. Mazc the Ishtel means Ishtels are the new royalty. Imagine it—all the statues and like-nesses towering over the city will have changed to great figures with thin lips."

She wriggled her lips at the king. "Don't laugh too quickly!" she cautioned, although his expression had not changed a bit. "We won't make statues of Ishtels. The same slaves who built all this will make rubble of your figures and your temple."

Varial had been working her toes into the wet grass, listening. "And what will you do with the king?" she asked. "It's customary for conquerors to bury royalty in the rubble."

Laren stood up and shook her head. "Someone has to take over the Ishtel's work. Who will care for the city's garbage if we now know Ishtels can do clever things? Surely the king and his officials would be much better at that than adding their bodies to the rubble of the temple."

Chapter 9.

A Soft Look? ——

Varial raised her eyebrows and cocked her head toward the next room where a priest was teaching Sanith about Askirit culture. "I don't like it."

Laren's own eyebrows rose and she puckered her chin. "Would you rather I had her wait on us like a servant?"

"I'd rather have her wait on the servants." Varial kept her voice low, but it had a hard edge. "Teach her, yes. But not here in your rooms."

The two women's eyes locked; Varial was always warning her. Since the fall of Belez, Mazcaen raiders had taken blood oaths, vowing to take Laren to their strongholds in the mountains, to sacrifice her there and regain their powers. They hated her above all—this Ishtel "queen," this unspeakable corruption who had destroyed their kingdom.

"I have news you won't like," Varial said.

"What now?"

Varial told her the Mazcaen king had escaped, that raiders had penetrated Belez and spirited him into the mountains. "Laren, the criticism will be quick and savage. But don't flinch."

She was painfully aware that most Askirit felt she should have executed the king. That angered her. "How can they forget who toppled Belez?"

Varial nodded and said, "Or how panicked they were when Bren was killed."

Even when Varial didn't agree with her, Laren was grateful she always shared the responsibility. But now the Enre's voice regained its hard edge. "Why have a Mazcaen princess right here in your chambers? Who knows what she's thinking?"

Laren ignored the question and, instead, signaled a guard. Before long a woman entered, Meleden cradled in her arms. Laren motioned for her to take the child to Sanith in the next room. A sour look flashed across the woman's face, then was gone as she moved to obey. Laren leaned against the doorway, studying the girl with the red, carefully tended curls rising from her chair to face the woman.

Stone-faced, Sanith put out her arms as the weighty child was laid into them. She awkwardly adjusted the baby's head beneath her chin, the baby's feet dangling at Sanith's waist.

The Mazcaen girl's thin body looked as if it would tip over any moment, her face sullen, as if she had been given a preposterous task. Laren kept watching her. "You can sit down with Meleden," she called across the room. "Make yourself comfortable with her."

Sanith refused to even acknowledge her suggestion; she braced her feet as if to steady herself. Finally, Laren walked across the room and lifted Meleden into her own arms, hoisting her head onto her shoulder and patting her back. "I thought you might like to hold her for a moment."

The girl gave a barely perceptible dip of her head.

After Sanith left, Laren said to Varial, "I'm trying to catch that look on her face that I saw there once, when she thought she was alone with Meleden. She was stooped over her crib, softness in her eyes."

"But rebellion there now."

"Yet as she released Meleden to me, I noticed one thing. I saw her squeeze her shoulder as she let her go."

Varial made a doubtful look with her mouth. Meleden was restlessly churning her legs and Laren eased back deeper into the chair, patting her. "Part of Sanith is drawn to the child. That's why she's here."

—— Home ——

Laren sat in pre-dawn darkness under a stand of trees near kelerai. Meleden was in her arms. Like Queen Mela before her, she had chosen Kelerai as her capital, and every morning she was here to greet the magnificent phenomenon. She saw against the night sky outlines of sentries and guards, all poised to protect her. She had refused to stay closeted in safety; as Varial herself had said, none should be hostage to the world's evil. Instead, think about the light.

She saw dawn starting to spread on the horizon, slowly brightening the sky, and then the slightest rim of red as colors started to spread toward her. Somehow, holding Meleden as she watched made everything more vivid. She wondered if the child understood anything at all about the rays starting to light up her face. Or did Meleden somehow see more of the dawn than Laren did? Holding Meleden as the skies were illumined with colors and drama made Laren feel as if she were not just seeing the sunrise but was plunging into it as into waves of the sea.

Meleden turned her head slightly toward the light as it revealed trees and hills and the royal buildings. Kelerai was soon to begin its rumblings when Laren noticed Sanith walking toward her, carrying something in her arms. Guards trailed her closely, for no one trusted her, least of all the guards assigned to her.

Many times afterward Laren tried to remember the exact sequence of these moments, for the drama playing out before her seemed to happen in some other place, to other people. Sanith had nearly reached her. Kelerai began, building greater and greater power, and at the instant it burst from the ground, she heard shouts. Laren looked from the exploding cascades to the sentries and realized that assassins had, at the moment of eruption when all eyes were on kelerai, struck at the men guarding her. Though Askirit soldiers were ringed around her, the raiders slashed down one then another in a precise assault, each Mazcaen a frenzy of motion and battle cries.

Strangely, though jolts of fear coursed through her, she was almost detached, evaluating her own physical responses and the battle surging toward her. She saw Sanith huddled in a ball on the ground; ten guards stood tight together in front of her, and then the fighting crashed into these men. Three assassins suddenly broke free and sprinted toward her.

Gripping Meleden in her left arm, she hefted her short sword grimly and swung at the first one who reached her. He easily dodged, for she was off balance holding the child, and the man grabbed her shoulder, yanking her sprawling into the hands of the others. She felt Meleden pulled away from her and she screamed.

Waking up, Laren struggled to make sense of where she was. Images of sacrifices made her want to escape back into her dreams; she did not want to awaken to Mazcaen horrors. Finally she opened her eyes, and as they focused, saw by the fabric beside her face that she was in her own bed.

Knees bent and legs splayed out above the rest of her, she was propped up by pillows, a brace holding both legs tight. Her left arm was free, and she moved it to her face where her jaw hurt. Her right cheekbone felt numb, a dull ache radiating from it into her eye.

Varial's hand carefully touched her shoulder. "They missed their chance."

Laren's jaw made her words come out wispy and garbled. "What about Meleden?"

Varial dabbed with a cloth at her mouth. "Like you—banged up. They could have killed you both if they'd tried right away. But they wanted to drag you to their altars. By then, we were on them."

Laren tried to thank her as Varial adjusted the bedclothes, but then the Enre said that they were interrogating Sanith.

"What?"

"You saw her coming directly toward you. At the very least, it was suspicious; most think she was showing them just where you were."

Laren was not surprised. "What does she say?"

"She had a perfectly good excuse—which means nothing."

"What excuse?"

"She was bringing you something." Varial wryly showed her teeth. "Tell me, when was the last time Sanith brought you something?"

Laren swallowed, and it hurt her throat. "Just don't interrogate her as the pagans do." She felt herself falling back asleep and feared returning to her dreams. But as she faded back into the softness beneath her, she encountered none of her nightmares.

Several days later, Laren was regaining her strength, but Meleden was not. Always frail, her injuries seemed to be draining her strength. After dinner, when they brought the child to her, both Varial and Gresen followed Galial as she carried her into the room. The child was weakly crying and twisting, as if seeking relief.

"She's not in a good way," Galial said, as if apologizing for the intrusion. "Sometimes she breathes as if she's desperate. She cries and can't be comforted. I really don't know how this child stays alive."

Laren motioned for her to lay her beside her on the bed. "Meleden is always dying." She said this to lighten their spirits, for it was a common saying about Meleden. Somehow it was a comfort, to say the words out loud, as if to keep it from happening.

Gresen, her arms bent like knobby sticks, was stroking her wet face. "It's like someone else breathes for her and keeps her here."

After a time Meleden quieted a bit and Galial said, "See, even when she's still, she hardly gets an easy breath."

Varial was standing at the window, singing. Laren looked over at her; she had never heard her sing before. It was a lilting, lively tune with no words, just child sounds of animals and sea birds and winds.

Gresen looked over at her and said, "That's odd. That same song has been going though my head too."

"What is it?" Laren asked.

"I have no idea," Gresen said. "I've never heard it before."

Laren felt Meleden's restless body beside her and, as she looked at her face, thought that despite her suffering, there was also a strange energy. This child who could say nothing and communicate nothing somehow radiated a peace even in her suffering.

Gresen had joined Varial in singing, and the sounds made Laren smile.

Then the bed was no longer moving beside her; the labored breathing was still. Laren twisted her head; Meleden lay quiet beside her.

Galial said, "She's gone."

Laren studied her little face, still shining with perspiration. "It doesn't seem remotely possible—not after all we've been through together." They were nearly nose to nose on the bed, and Laren had to arc her arm to stroke her soft, wet skin. "She's gone home. But she left behind a fragrance."

"And a song," said Varial.

Horses

A wondrous celebration had welcomed Bren, celestials and friends and loved ones embracing him, full of stories and explanations as he had walked among them over a rolling mossy plain with tree-edged pools and clear springs. The celebration had gone on and on.

One of the celestials, intrigued by Asta's mysteries, had asked him many questions. Then the shining messenger, huge legs splashing through a shallow pool, had looked over and asked, "Is this where you came through?"

Bren looked around, seeing many pools. "I don't know."

The celestial jumped from the pool and grabbed his shoulders. "Stand here—yes, closer," and he pulled Bren forward. "Stand and look. See the sparkles? Look carefully—you have to get just the right angle."

Bren stood where he was placed, cocking his head, and eventually saw sparkles of many colors—colors new to his eyes and mind.

"It's a seam. See, I'll stick my arm into it." The celestial's arm disappeared, and he stood with only a stump under his iridescent shoulder. "My fingers are wriggling in another world."

Suddenly he jerked his arm back. "It's not the time to come and go," he announced, as if he had just heard a command. "But your other world is right here. I mean, close as that tree." He made an expansive gesture with his arms. "But not just one world. An infinity of worlds. And each one a universe."

Since that conversation, Bren had seen several more souls welcomed at this spring, with music and dancing and, especially for one lively old man, great hilarity. Yet now, as he watched a growing commotion around it and felt the heightening excitement, he sensed something extraordinary even for this place was about to happen. Swirls of celestials and people were rushing toward the spring. Sparkles had begun flaring out of the seam in a narrow line that rose to the sky.

Suddenly, as he watched, he saw the noses of horses above the celebrants breaking through the line of sparkling colors. The next instant a stampede of horses triumphantly galloped through the seam. Half were ebony black, the other half milk white. Their manes and tails were brightly aflame, and on the back of each horse rode a celestial.

A tiny figure sat on the shoulders of a great white horse, balanced there by a strong supporting arm of a shining one. The horses stomped onto the moss, raced round and round the spring, and finally came to a nickering, sweaty stop.

Bren knew instantly the little figure was Meleden. She was eased from the horse's back and stood, straight and sturdy beside the great creature, barely reaching to his knee.

As he watched the little girl, he felt something nuzzling his back. He turned to see a magnificent black horse, its mane and tail flaming. Sensing the horse had been sent to him, he grabbed its flaming mane and held it strong in his fist as he yanked himself aboard.

The horse cantered toward the celebration at the spring; Bren watched Meleden looking wide-eyed around her, greeting the morning. Like creatures who shed skins and emerge fresh yet the same, it was as if she had shed layers of the infirm Meleden and was now just as much herself, but fully aware and able.

The child spied Mela, her mother, and began running exuberantly across the green-and-purple moss. She crashed into Mela's outstretched arms, and they fell down laughing, with her father joining the mêlée.

The horse brought Bren closer. He felt a special awe. This was Mela, his queen, romping with the child he also loved.

He slipped off the horse, and Mela's face lighted up in recognition. She got up from the moss, and Meleden leaped into her arms, a light burden full of life. Throwing her free arm around Bren, Mela drew him into their circle.

The child hiked herself higher, one hand on a shoulder of each, and looked right at Bren. "I know you." She was looking at him with great satisfaction. "You rescued me."

Bren turned to Mela. "How could she know that?"

She hoisted her daughter into Bren's arms. "She has long been at the very heart of the Maker, learning unknown things. And everywhere it's whispered that she has arrived just in time—for Auret has a task for her."

Part Three

*You will find wonders only new eyes can see;
you will span worlds only new bodies can enter.*

—THE ASKIRIT LITURGY

Chapter 10.

—— Cataclysm ——

Laren lay on her litter under the stand of trees near kelerai, the guards doubled around her. Dawn was breaking and kelerai about to begin. She saw Josk pacing on the grounds, keeping his head aimed so he could watch the geysers erupt.

Poor old Josk. All he could think of were the prophecies of their world's fiery end. All through Mela's reign he had fretted, and now in hers. To Josk, the new quakes were ominous, and the end was surely overdue.

Something suddenly shifted under her. Pebbles from somewhere above clattered to the ground next to her feet. She stretched forward to look at them but then felt kelerai begin its rumblings.

Laren thought the start of the geysers might have somehow caused the strange shifting she still felt beneath her, but then the moment kelerai burst from the ground, its rumblings grew louder. Much louder.

Louder? They should be starting to subside, Laren thought. Yet they were shaking her legs. Her fingers dug into the litter poles as the shaking increased, as if a giant dog were whipping her back and forth. The ground split between her and the great widening cascades rushing upwards. Suddenly she was hit by water that plunged her down, then moments later lifted her as a powerful reverberation sounded through her body. She was spun and torn and flung free as the entire planet exploded into the void.

And then Laren was above it, seeing below trees bursting into flames and water hissing, debris blasting up as her body disintegrated with the shattering of the planet but her soul kept streaking upward.

Then everything blinked out, and she was standing by a river, one much like the river in Belez. She looked around. A mountain rose nearby as majestic as the one she had stared at every day of her childhood. But there was no city.

A voice called to her. "Well done."

Somehow, she knew instantly it was Auret. He was standing like an ordinary man at the river's edge, beckoning for her to come down to him.

"Welcome home, Laren. Yes, home. All of this is now yours."

She looked into Auret's face and saw the father she had always longed for. "All those you love will come to you here— Meleden and Bren, Varial and Gresen.. . ."

Home. She'd spoken of Meleden's "going home," but now she felt the depth of those words. Not just that these were her native skies but that Auret was welcoming her and that she was now intimately connected with all those he loved.

"You belong. And you will make a great city here, a place of light and joy."

Safely home. She felt the first pulses of new energies, the old anxieties leaching away.

Laren noticed marks on Auret's face and was reminded of all the stories of how he had gone to the depths of Aliare's darkness, had suffered and been cast into the deadly pit.

He smiled, for he knew her thoughts. "You're wondering why I went through all that? I did it for you. For this moment of joy, and for countless moments to come. I will never leave you— not even a little, though you will often be elsewhere, discovering the vastness of life."

High in the air, toward the mountains, she saw scintillating light rushing toward them. "Come. They are waiting to celebrate with you. Those who love you wait on tiptoes for your coming."

—— A Withered Little Soul ——

Sanith stood at the window of her room. Guards posted at her door never gave her a pleasant word, for they were convinced she had betrayed their queen.

They were right. She had aimed the assassins directly toward Laren. She had wanted the Ishtel dead.

The girl was watching the dawn and kelerai's eruption when the shaking began and the massive plumes began widening. The floor shook violently, and as she fell, it buckled beneath her. She hurtled down between collapsing timbers, swallowed up as the entire structure fell into a wide crack.

Instants later her body was propelled upward from the explosions beneath, but she herself was floating in darkness, a withered little soul spinning aimlessly.

During the past several days, feeling the condemnation around her, she had drawn on all her old hatreds. Yet she knew Laren had loved her, and most of all she longed for the love that kept springing alive whenever she was near Meleden. She had spoken to the sleeping child, quietly, when no one was listening. She had even called out to the Auret they always spoke of, that he would silence the vile accusations within her and give her some peace.

But then Meleden was dead, and all Sanith's silent cries to the child had rocked back at her like echoes from an empty canyon.

I am dead, she thought, spinning alone. *What terrors of death will come for me?* Her royal identity melted away; she saw herself being thrown into harsh labor like an Ishtel or being sacrificed again and again on dark altars. Or would she suddenly cease to exist?

Then she saw a small circle of light below. It grew and grew until she was inside it, her feet on a curved, golden walkway.

In the center of a thick bank of flowers nearby stood a little girl, looking at her. Despite the flowers and the girl, Sanith was full of fear—until she realized the girl was Meleden. The once-infirm child hopped out of the flowers and scampered down the walkway toward her. Radiance poured from her skin; the same golden light radiated from the flowers and leaves and from a bird flying past.

Meleden's face was intelligent, "knowing" in a disconcerting way, yet she made no sound. She simply grasped Sanith's hand, a large smile on her face, and started leading her up the walkway past the flowers toward a tall white building.

Holding Meleden's hand was like plunging hers into a lively brook; it gave her entire being new energy. But far more than mere energy, her touching and seeing Meleden brought back that powerful sense of love she feared she had lost forever.

She wondered how long Meleden had been here, and the child flowed answers into her mind: This is home. I've *always* been here.

Sanith sensed Meleden had long been loved and nurtured. Though the child's thoughts were simple, they were also wise, and Sanith felt shriveled and childish as her thoughts mixed with hers.

Up golden stairs and through huge doorways sparkling with jewels and across a great hall they went, until she saw at the far end a man sitting on a high throne. Sanith stopped suddenly, blinking her eyes, almost making Meleden tumble forward. "Who is that?" The man was formed of tiny golden circles pulsing like suns, yet she could look right at him.

"You called out to him once. Don't you remember?" Meleden's arms were raised high above her head in triumph.

The man stepped down and started walking toward them, his radiance lighting the vast hall. When he reached them, he scooped both into his arms, and as he held them, Sanith noticed her own arm around his neck was luminous with the same radiance pouring from his body.

The Sea

An instant after Varial's body was crushed in Asta's destruction, she felt her bare feet on submerged rocks, waves breaking over her ankles so strongly that she leaned forward to keep from tipping over. She braced against the winds whipping her long hair, dark clouds on the horizon rolling toward her. She loved the drama of stormy weather.

Ribbons of light rippled in the water beneath—glowing fish aiming toward shore. With her rigorous Enre sea training, she plunged in among them, swimming energetically as they nosed beside her in shimmering waves and shot in front of her, as if to urge her on.

Halfway to shore, she spied a lone man hunched over a fire. Closer in, she smelled fish cooking. By the time she rose dripping on the shore, her lively appetite had awakened.

It was Auret. He stood and offered her some. She began to kneel before him, but he simply sat down beside her. She took a piece from his hand, her fingers sliding over his. How natural it seemed to be with him.

She ate and thought, The fish was caught and died. But I thought death was abolished here.

Auret entered her mind: The fish gave its life, but nothing is lost.

He walked into the water, waited a moment, then with a quick motion grabbed a fish from the water. He brought it to her flopping in his hand. It grew still, and, as its eyes glazed, she saw emerging from it a translucent, winged creature which reminded her of a thin blue heron, far more beautiful than the fish. It flew off, and she could not tell if it was still flying in this world or into another, for it suddenly disappeared.

"What will happen to the bird? Will it also some day die?"

"Nothing will be lost," Auret said. "But you are like us. You are eternal. Your old body, spread out in space with the debris of that unstable world, was simply seed." He handed her another piece of fish. "You'll find your new body even more satisfactory that the first. There are many changings, but the love of the Maker never changes."

"And all the darkness and evil we experienced in Asta?"

"I was always hovering over the chaos. I was always making out of the wreckage things new and wondrous."

Rags

Galial found herself floating through some sort of dark canyon, then walking by a bubbling, narrow brook. She still felt the terror of her moments before death as her body fell into the gaping, shaking ground.

Far ahead she saw a small glow. She stopped walking, fearing the purity of light and all she had heard of its power. Her hypocrisies made her feel like a beast; how could anyone as dirty as she stand the light? The stories of Auret in his power and glory, lifted high in light unthinkable, terrified her more than the kings of Belez, who with one withering look would send the guilty to the torturers.

Galial felt guilty. She felt ashamed and sordid.

On the other side of the stream, a man in rags was bent over, busy at some task. An Ishtel here to accuse me, she thought—here to condemn me. But why? I befriended an Ishtel once.

The man turned to face her. "I know." He was smiling, his face filled with light, and she knew he was Auret.

He wore the scars of old wounds, and she remembered the stories of his descent into darkness to confront evil. "Why are you dressed like an Ishtel?"

"These are just rags. I've often worn them. Rags of the beaten, the refugees, the slaves." He smiled again. "You were one once." The light of his face did not terrify her. Instead, it was cleansing her, filling her with power and love.

In his hand he held a delicate golden hoop, a large earring of the kind a groom gives to his bride. He who was beyond time and place reached across the little brook and placed it into her hand. "Put it on. It designates purity and honor."

She put it on her right ear; it dangled nearly to her neck. Then he motioned her toward the light further down the stream.

Galial ran lightly along the brook toward the light and came to a little bridge. On the other side, out of the darkness, she saw burning eyes, and then bright, luminous faces. Halfway across the bridge she recognized they were her friends, Gresen, Varial, Laren and others, their faces lighting up the huge window by the open door of a stately yet inviting home.

Little Meleden bolted through the doorway and began running toward her. Galial heard the brook beneath bubbling and leaping like the new spirit within her. As she looked at her friends approaching, faces alive with radiance and deep intelligence, she ran toward them and scooped Meleden up in her arms.

The Fertile Void

On a bluff overlooking a vast city, Bren watched a man standing vigorous as a stallion, fierce and joyous, nostrils flaring, palms flung upward. It was Josk, praying for the city.

Bren came close to him and joined in his prayers, participating in the ecstasy and wonder of drawing the Maker's holy energies into the busy lives of those below. Bren prayed with him for a long time until Josk turned and said, "How could we ever have thought that prayer was a stifling burden?"

Bren said, "We're becoming more and more like him."

"For cosmic purposes beyond imagination."

A dazzling celestial materialized beside them, twice Bren's size and looking cosmic indeed. He was full of good humor, having heard them, and said it was beyond their imagination what Bren would soon be doing. "The Maker always makes all things new," the great one said, and Bren suddenly found himself floating in space with him, not even a star to be seen. The celestial made an expansive gesture with his arm. "A fresh nothingness! A universe to be started. Cosmic purposes unimaginable."

A bar of green light appeared under Bren's feet. He balanced himself on it. He leaned over and gripped it with both hands; it was substantial yet soft and translucent. Yellow struts began extending downward from the bar, supporting the green triangle forming beneath him. The triangles proliferated. They honeycombed into rolling fields of green-and-yellow light starting to stretch as far as he could see.

Hills and valleys of harmonious colors were being formed, and the celestial said, "It is Auret. It is the Spirit. It is the Maker. And it is your hands and mine." He ran his fingers down Bren's arm and flung it sideways. Brown, triangular mounds full of light rose up from the green.

"Everything new," the celestial said. "New physics. New mysteries. New ways of love among new creatures—but all full of the Maker's intent and pleasures. Here will appear creatures unimagined."

The celestial disappeared.

Bren spun around, looking at the horizons of this fresh, expanding world, alien yet beautiful and inviting. He sensed the fecund force of light shaping and creating. And he knew he was central to all this.

Flickers of brightness on a hill drew his attention. Radiance shimmered toward him over the new terrain, making him think it was another celestial. Then, as it came closer, he began to see airy, flowing garments, revealing a feminine form and glorious, familiar, golden hair. He began running exuberantly toward the woman, surprised by the great leaps his legs were making on this world aborning.

The effect of actually seeing Laren in front of him—running with equal enthusiasm toward him—was remarkably akin to how he had responded to her in his former body. On Asta, her face and hair and frightened little smile had awakened a longing to talk to her, to touch her, to merge body and soul. Now, she looked far more stunning than before, fully as feminine and desirable, and the effect was even greater, a continuity of awakened longings. Yet it was also completely different. His eyes saw her in different dimensions and forms, his emotions unsullied and powerful, his being full of the same light radiating from her.

He remembered a celestial's words: "On old Asta, they couldn't handle the wild, untamed force of sex. Cut off from the Source, they'd lost the awe and holiness of a man beholding his naked bride. But here the wildness comes from the One who is energy and love and light, unpredictable, with holy sensuality."

Laren's face was bright laughter as they rushed together, connecting in a swirling dance with thoughts mixing like rushing surf. She was iridescent, yet flesh—new flesh, and their minglings in magnificent dance became more pure and ecstatic than could have been imagined by mortals. The rhythms of their thoughts were as passionate as their bodies, celebrating the new hungers of mind and body the Maker had placed within them.

They celebrated the many challenges the Maker was giving them. They had entered the great harmony, in which no restrictions of time or task would limit their freedom to be obedient.

——— The Feast ———

Bren loved listening to the tales around the fire. Laren was there, and Varial, Gresen, Tatt, and Leas. Mela the queen was there, with many she loved, and their ancestors that Auret had led from darkness—Yosha, Asel, Maachah—all in new, vigorous bodies.

He stood close to the fire, watching its orange tongues leaping like dancers into the air. Here, all was light, the flames complementing the radiance of their bodies. He passed his hand though the fire; its lively warmth mingled with the remarkable energies in his wrist and fingers.

"When we were in the darkness of Aliare," Yosha said, "where we struck sparks to keep our eyes alive, Auret came as a child—crushed by more than the storms. He confronted the dark powers. He brought us the light."

The celestials among them hunched closer, anxious to hear the tales, the marvels of how Auret himself had fallen into the scorched, hollowed world, battered and humiliated but somehow rescuing these sons and daughters, these mortals now immortal.

"He brought us out of the wreckage," Asel said, "and each of us is a tale." Then Asel told her story, some of which Laren had heard from Bren but not with such detail and depth. Yosha then told all his adventures, and there was no hurry in the telling.

Everyone shared their stories, but they were all Auret's tales, for the radiance in their faces was from him.

The one they spoke of was suddenly among them, but he did not appear in his glory. He was simply walking toward them across a meadow, surrounded by lively children. He talked and played with them, throwing one after another so high into the air Laren marveled at his strength and, had she been in Asta, would have feared for the child. But here there was no fear, and when one radiant boy in his exuberance spun crazily out of Auret's hand and landed flat on the side of his head, he simply rose laughing and Auret flung him into the air again.

Laren noticed Meleden as just one bobbing head among the other children, but then she was among the adults, running from one to the other, landing in Laren's arms with a spirited whoop, a gripping hug, a few words, and then off. Laren marveled at the full person Meleden had become, yet still a child, growing and experiencing the joys of childhood, but here, none of the pains.

Others appeared, all sorts of celestials and remarkable creatures of every shape and size, clothing and adornments wonderfully diverse, each with a unique identity. They had come to dance and sing and praise, and they moved to a grove of trees by the river where they feasted on thick, ripe orbs of fruit.

And then the man with the children stepped out on the rippling river, standing on it as if it were a meadow, and lifted Meleden high above his head. All eyes were fixed on him. "I chose this child before the worlds were made. Chose her to touch you. She brought life to many, for she was always in my arms and in my heart." He lowered her and kissed her cheek. "She is beloved."

Laren felt a hand on her shoulder, then arms tightly embracing her. It was Sanith, her face full of joy. "I'm here because of Meleden," she said. "But also because of you. If you hadn't seen that look in my eyes—if you hadn't hoped for me despite my betraying you—I'd be cut off from all this." She shook her head as if that were unthinkable. "You kept me near the child of love."

Mela had seen her daughter Meleden with the other children, and when her lively little girl had bounded up to her and landed on her lap, she had hugged her very tightly, full of joyful tears. Long, long ago she had held Meleden limp and unaware for so many nights; now Mela was still adjusting to seeing her lively and talking. When Meleden bolted away, her mother's heart kept reaching for her, even when she was being held aloft by Auret and he was calling her little daughter beloved. She remembered that remarkable moment long ago in the depths of Aliare when Auret had called her beloved. She felt united with both of them, especially when Auret motioned for Mela to come up to them, and he embraced them together.

But then Meleden bounded off again; Mela wondered what more she could possibly ask than her daughter's joy and wholeness. Yet she also remembered with deep longing the hours she had spent holding the helpless child, and that powerful bond of love for the dependent yet powerful newborn.

Mela's father, Steln, had been reading her feelings and thoughts. "Mela, your longings remind me of my own."

She turned and saw in his hands a clump of tiny, delicate flowers. "When you were a little girl, I loved to be with you. You were full of life, yet blindness brought bitter pain. And then you were gone, and I was longing to be with you."

His nostalgia struck a deep, resonating chord in her. "And I with you." Mela was drawn into his mind: images of putting flowers into her hair and exploring islands and talking under stars.

Her father said, "The new-born Meleden is a memory. Like you, when you were a child." Then he said, as if offering her a wondrous gift, "Yet . . . we can go back."

She asked what he meant.

"We have no limits here. We can newly live the best times, fully communing with the Maker. Here, your desires are His. Everything you long for can be."

Into her mind flowed strange, thrilling opportunities, mixing past, present, future in ways mysteriously one, ways she could never have understood in her mortal body.

They willed in His will, and they were instantly alone together by the sea where she once played. She was again the same little girl, but no longer blind; alive with the vividness of childhood, yet also aware of the new realities. The smell of the sea filled her nostrils and her emotions.

"Nothing of the best is lost," Steln said. "All can be forever savored. We can stay as long as we wish." And the father and the little girl Mela stepped into a boat, full of anticipation, and headed toward a little island they had walked so long ago.

——— Glory ———

The vast city of light appeared as a glow in the distance, growing rapidly larger, as if moving toward them. "Are we traveling toward it, or it toward us?" Bren asked the celestial escorting him.

"Both."

The city rushed toward them, extremely bright. Bren felt he was staring into the sun, but he could look right at it and the magnificent creatures full of eyes and wings and power, constantly moving in exuberant yet solemn worship.

Rushing toward him, the celestials lifted him like a leaf and tossed him from one to another, amid thunderings of millions of voices full of praise. Indescribable music reverberated through him, as if every grain of matter in the infinity of universes had found voice.

The celestial with him became a ball of light and hurtled away. Many such living spheres of fire wheeled, circled and swept past the deepest glory where Auret was.

Bren stood before the magnificence, filled with the harmony, all creatures bound together in the Maker's love.

As they hurtled toward the city of light, the celestial with Laren said, "You who come from the darkness were made more like Auret than us all. You sought him when the enemy came."

Laren stared at the brilliance of the approaching glory. "Auret fills all of space," the celestial said, "he holds every charge of it together. Yet he also rests and laughs and redeems. Nothing limits him, except when he becomes weak for us." The celestial began singing stories of Auret's times of helplessness, and others joined her, passing them like precious gems from one to another.

As they sped toward the brightest rays of the city, Laren thought of Auret embracing Meleden and knew it was wonderfully congruent with his glory. Everywhere voices were raised in exultant worship, singing, "Splendor. Wonder. Majesty."

And those redeemed from the wreckage of the dark planet joined in recounting his magnificent deeds, singing,

Glory! Glory! Glory!
Glory forever and forever.

Glossary

Aliàre—the nightworld beneath the planet's surface inhabited by
   Askirit, their enemies the Laij, and various tribes
Asta—the world above
aurets—birds in Aliare that symbolize morning; also called
   dawnbreakers

Enre—ancient Askirit religious order of women warriors

Ishtel—white, "mouth slit in washed-out face," blue eyes,
   freckles, finely chiseled little nose

kelerai—spectacular, massive geysers which erupt each morning
   in Asta
Kelerai—the small city near the place where the kelerai geysers
   erupt
keitr—poisonous, batlike creatures in the nightworld, gathered by
   the Askirit from caves and fired at enemies with deadly
   effect

sierent—the daily, immense upheaval of underground waters; the
   time period people in Aliare call night

Varial—leader of the Enre

Yette—the Askirit tactile language consisting of intricate motions
   of fingers on another's skin